FROM THE
NANCY DREW FILES

THE CASE: Nancy makes a new circle of friends . . .
and ends up facing a ring of jewel thieves.

CONTACT: Claudia Beluggi takes Nancy on a tour of
the city, which leads into the heart of a Roman
mystery.

SUSPECTS: Massimo Bianco—his specialty is fake
Etruscan jewelry . . . but is he an art student or a
con artist?

Paola Rinzini—she sells Massimo's costume jewelry in her boutique . . . but is she conducting a
more lucrative—and illegal—trade on the side?

Fabio Andreotti—he is a dealer in antiquities, but
is he dealing in deception as well?

COMPLICATIONS: Sparks are flying between Bess
and Massimo, but is it romance . . or a Roman
candle? If Nancy implicates him in the theft, the
fireworks are sure to start.

Books in The Nancy Drew Files® Series

Available from ARCHWAY Paperbacks

The Nancy Drew Files™

PASSPORT TO ROMANCE #2

Case 73
Rendezvous in Rome

Carolyn Keene

AN ARCHWAY PAPERBACK
Published by POCKET BOOKS

New York London Toronto Sydney Tokyo Singapore

AN ARCHWAY PAPERBACK *Original*

An Archway Paperback published by
POCKET BOOKS, a division of Simon & Schuster Inc.
1230 Avenue of the Americas, New York, NY 10020

Copyright © 1992 by Simon & Schuster Inc.
Produced by Mega-Books of New York, Inc.

ISBN: 0-671-73077-0

First Archway Paperback printing July 1992

10 9 8 7 6 5 4 3 2 1

NANCY DREW, AN ARCHWAY PAPERBACK and colophon
are registered trademarks of Simon & Schuster Inc.

THE NANCY DREW FILES is a trademark
of Simon & Schuster Inc.

Cover art by Tricia Zimic

Printed in the U.S.A.

IL 6+

Rendezvous in Rome

Chapter

One

"YOU LOOK TERRIFIC!" Claudia Beluggi exclaimed. She planted a kiss on each of Nancy Drew's cheeks, then did the same to Nancy's best friends, George Fayne and Bess Marvin. "Don't tell me you three got those tans in Geneva!"

George squinted into the sunlight and lifted her short, dark curls off her neck. "Actually, we took a detour on our way down from Geneva and stopped on the Italian Riviera," she explained.

"Well, you will *not* relax here," Claudia said, her black eyes glowing merrily. "Last night, when you called from your pensione, I promised I would show you every inch of Rome, and I mean it!"

Nancy grinned at the tall, slender girl. Claudia's long, wavy black hair looked great against the royal blue of her fitted minidress, and her warm smile was the same as Nancy remembered. Next to Claudia, Nancy's khaki shorts, cotton tank top, and sneakers seemed very . . . American.

She, Bess, and George had met Claudia at an outdoor concert in Geneva at the beginning of their summer vacation in Europe. They had hit it off immediately with the bubbly Italian girl. When Claudia suggested that they spend some time in Rome, they had jumped at the chance.

"This place is great," Nancy said now, looking around Piazza Navona, where she and her friends had come to meet Claudia. She had read in her guidebook that it was one of Rome's most popular hangouts. Laughter and conversations in different languages buzzed around them as crowds surged past. A lot of people had cameras and were obviously tourists, but there were also many groups of young people who were speaking Italian.

Bess nodded her agreement. "All these carved stone buildings are so much fancier and older than what we have at home. And your language sounds so romantic!" She giggled and added, "Too bad I can't understand a word of it."

"That is the Fountain of the Four Rivers, by Bernini," Claudia said, seeing George staring at the magnificent stone fountain at the center of the piazza. Four huge stone figures towered over the crowd. It was balanced at both ends of the piazza by smaller fountains.

"Pretty impressive," George commented.

Bess's gaze had strayed to a string of street artists and craftspeople who had set up displays in the piazza. "Hey, check it out," she said. The vendors vied for the girls' attention, calling out as they walked along.

"If you want to shop, a good friend of mine makes unusual jewelry and sells it here," Claudia told her. "Come, I will show you."

The girls followed Claudia, pausing to inspect the jewelry and crafts at the stands they passed. Ornate gold jewelry hung from velvet boards on one of the tables, catching the light. Nancy leaned forward, admiring the intricate designs on the beads of one of the necklaces.

"Prego?" a deep voice spoke into Nancy's ear. *"Parla italiano?"*

"Yes. I mean, *sì,"* Nancy replied in Italian. When she turned toward the person who had offered to help her, she straightened in delight.

The young man was taller than average, and Nancy had to tilt her head up to look at his face. His wide, toothy smile stood out against his golden skin, and his raven eyes matched the color of his black, wavy hair exactly. He was gorgeous!

"Massimo!" Claudia kissed the young man on both cheeks with gusto. "Meet some new friends." She turned to the girls. "Massimo Bianco, this is Nancy Drew, George Fayne, and Bess Marvin."

"Nice to meet you," Massimo said. When he saw Bess, his eyes lit up. Swiftly he bent and kissed her on both cheeks.

"That is how we greet friends in Rome," he explained, his eyes dancing.

Nancy stifled a grin as Bess's face turned pink. Usually Bess was a complete flirt, but it looked as if she had met her match in Massimo.

"Massimo is an artist," Claudia explained. "He made all this jewelry."

"A student artist," Massimo corrected. "I sell what I can in the summer and study the rest of the year." His words flowed in a melodic Italian accent.

Bess was busy looking at a row of beaded gold-tone necklaces pinned to the velvet display. "Your work is very beautiful," she commented. "Are they original designs?"

"Actually, the Etruscans made the designs first," Massimo told her. "I just copy them from museums. The originals are more than two thousand years old."

"The Etruscans?" Nancy repeated. She tried to think back to her European history class but drew a blank. "Who are they?"

"They lived in Tuscany in ancient times, before the Roman Empire came into being," Claudia told the girls. "They were masters at jewelry-making, and with gold in particular."

Massimo handed Bess a mirror and held one of the necklaces lightly against her neck. "It is perfect," he said with satisfaction. "The blue stones match your eyes exactly."

The necklace consisted of long and short gold-toned beads. Blue stones flashed in each of the three center beads, which were set off on either side by two longer, oblong beads that looked to Nancy like some kind of fruit. Two types of smaller beads—small rosettes and beads covered in a sandy-textured finish—alternated to fill out the rest of the necklace.

"Wow," Nancy commented. "That's beautiful."

"I'll say," Bess agreed. Smiling up at Massimo, she said, "I'll take it. But you said it's fake, right? You won't charge me all the money I have, will you?"

Massimo slipped the necklace into a paper bag and handed it to her. "Do you dance?" he asked without answering her question.

Bess wrinkled her nose and looked puzzled as she took the bag. "I love to dance. But what does that have to do—"

"Then dance with me, and the necklace is yours," Massimo said, cutting off Bess's question.

"Here?" Bess looked around the bustling piazza.

Massimo shook his head. "Not here," he assured her. "But sometime before you leave Rome."

Bess started to protest, but Massimo held up a hand to stop her. "Nancy, George, you must pick something, too, so Bess will not argue."

George shook her head. "Your work is beautiful, but it's not my style."

To Nancy's surprise, Massimo nodded his agreement. "You are right," he said. "You need something simple but elegant. Perhaps in silver." He turned to Nancy. "And I think copper for you," he said, reaching out to touch her red-gold hair. "For your beautiful hair."

This guy is quite a charmer, Nancy thought, but he did seem nice, and Bess was certainly enjoying his compliments. "Bess, I think you'd better thank Massimo," Nancy said quickly, "and we should get moving. Otherwise we'll bankrupt this poor guy."

As another tourist came over to the display the girls said goodbye to Massimo and moved on.

"I think we will be seeing a lot more of Massimo," Claudia said as they reached the edge of the piazza. "We have been friends since we were children. He is really a great guy."

"Do you think he likes me?" Bess asked anxiously. "I mean, do all Italian guys treat girls that way? It's so romantic!"

"Here we go again," George whispered to Nancy. "He's a hunk. She's in love."

Claudia hooked her arm with Bess's and assured her, "He is not like that with every girl. I am sure he likes you."

"I know what's coming next," George said, trying to keep a straight face. Mimicking Bess's voice, she said, "He's *sooo* gorgeous!"

"Well, he is," Bess insisted as the other girls laughed.

"Speaking of romance," Claudia said, looking at Nancy, "what happened with that blond guy I saw you with in Geneva? His name was Mick, right?"

"Mick Devlin," George said, nodding. "The Australian mystery man who was after Nancy. We left him heartbroken in Geneva."

Nancy felt the familiar blush rising to her cheeks. It seemed to come over her whenever Mick's name came up. "We were really just good friends," she said.

Bess raised one eyebrow. "Very good friends,"

she said. More gently she added, "And from that dreamy look you get at the mention of his name, I think he's not the only one a little heartbroken."

A retort sprang to Nancy's lips, but she stifled it. She did miss Mick sometimes, she had to admit. It was more than just the few sizzling kisses they had shared. There was something about Mick that was really special. But she couldn't stay in Geneva just to see where the romance was going. Especially when she didn't even know where things stood with Ned Nickerson, her longtime boyfriend back home.

"Sorry I brought it up," Claudia said, giving Nancy a sympathetic smile. She changed the subject, saying, "I was thinking that we should go to via Condotti today. It is near the Spanish Steps and the hottest place to shop in Rome. I told Sandro we would meet him there for lunch."

"Sandro?" Nancy asked. "Another date for Bess?"

"I hope not," Claudia said indignantly. "Sandro Fiorello is *my* boyfriend."

Claudia guided the girls onto a bus, pointing out some of Rome's famous sights as they rode along. "You will love via Condotti," she said as the girls got off at their stop. "I work part-time here this summer in a store called Preziosi."

"Preziosi?" Nancy repeated. "That means precious, right? So I guess you must sell some really good stuff."

"Esattamente!" Claudia said, smiling. "But everything on via Condotti is worth seeing."

Claudia was right. Via Condotti was a wide,

cobbled street lined with Rome's most luxurious shops. Luscious leather goods and shoes caught the girls' eyes as they passed store windows. Even the shoppers seemed more elegant than the crowds the girls had seen at Piazza Navona.

"Look at that!" Bess said, stopping outside a shop window and pointing to a flared silk dress with bright geometric designs on it. "We have to go in there."

"Only if you want to spend a lot of money," Claudia warned. "The prices are outrageous. If you wait until we get to Preziosi, I can get you a discount on leather goods and beautiful accessories. We don't sell clothing, however."

The girls couldn't resist going inside the store. When the saleslady told Bess the price of the dress Nancy mentally converted the Italian lire to American dollars. Her mouth dropped open. "Bess, that's over four hundred dollars," she said in an undertone.

"Uh, thanks but no thanks," Bess said, hurriedly pulling her friends back out into the hot summer air. "From now on I'm just looking!"

A short while later Claudia stopped in front of an elegant stone doorway with a wrought-iron gate. "Here we are," she announced to Nancy, Bess, and George. She ushered the girls into a small boutique. Several glass cases of jewelry were placed against one wall, and scarves hung artistically from bars around the room. Leather items such as handbags, belts, and wallets were displayed on separate shelves opposite the jewelry.

"This is Maria," Claudia said, introducing Nancy, Bess, and George to a plump, middle-aged woman who was chatting on the telephone near the cashier. Keeping the telephone to her ear, the woman smiled and waved at the girls.

"Maria, aren't those new necklaces on display yet?" Claudia asked after taking a brief look at the jewelry cases. Maria shrugged and shook her head.

"I wanted to show you some more of Massimo's Etruscan necklaces," Claudia explained to the girls. "Sandro dropped them off for Massimo yesterday."

"Massimo sells his work at Preziosi?" Bess asked. "Looking at these prices, now I'm really embarrassed that I got my necklace for free."

Grinning at Bess, George said, "You must have really made an impression on him."

Claudia excused herself to go to the back room. "I thought Paola would have put them out, but I don't see them. They must still be in the back." She disappeared through a door against one wall.

"Look at these beautiful scarves!" Bess exclaimed, pulling a multicolored silk one from its hanger. She wrapped it over her head like a hood. "Do I look like a movie star?" she asked, batting her eyes dramatically.

"You would with these sunglasses," George offered, slipping a pair of sleek black frames onto Bess's face. "Actually, I might even buy a pair for myself. I lost my old ones on the Riviera, remember?"

The three girls looked over as Claudia returned from the back room with a package in her hand. "Here they are," she said, breaking the seal with her fingernail and letting three gold-tone necklaces spill out onto the glass counter. "Now, these are fabulous."

"Hey, this one looks almost like mine," Bess said, fingering a necklace with three blue stones. Reaching into her aqua knapsack, she quickly fished out the necklace Massimo had given her and put it on the counter next to the store's necklace.

"They really do look similar," George commented. She picked up the necklace and ran her finger over the bumpy surface of one of the beads. "How do they get this granular effect?"

"The Etruscans had a special method for putting grains of gold onto surfaces without melting them," Claudia said.

When George returned the necklace to the counter, Bess picked it up again and put it on. "Guys, do you like this and the scarf together?" she asked, surveying her reflection in the mirror.

Nancy came over, a pair of men's gloves in her hand. "Nice," she said. She turned to Claudia. "These leather gloves are as soft as butter. My dad would love them."

Bess decided to buy the scarf while George got the sunglasses. The girls paid for their purchases while Claudia returned the three necklaces to the back. Then, after saying goodbye to Maria, the four girls walked outside again.

"Perfect," George said, slipping on her new sunglasses. "Now I can face this hot Italian sun."

The girls walked lazily to the end of via

Condotti, where the street opened up into Piazza di Spagna and the Spanish Steps.

"This looks sort of familiar," Bess said, looking around. "Aren't we near our pensione?"

Claudia nodded and explained, "It's down that street to the left." Shading her eyes with her hand, she looked around the piazza. "Sandro should be here somewhere. Let's go to the top of the steps and see if we can spot him."

They picked their way through people perched with their lunches on the wide, curving stone steps. When they got to the top, Nancy found herself standing on the edge of another street lined with shops and hotels. From here she felt as if she could see the whole city. A carpet of red tile roofs stretched out before her, interspersed with church domes. The grand dome of St. Peter's Basilica floated on the horizon.

The piazza below was almost as crowded as Piazza Navona had been. Displays of flowers and crafts were set up haphazardly all around the oval area. And this piazza had a fountain, too, a long carved stone boat with water sheeting over the sides.

"There he is," Claudia said, pointing.

Nancy saw a young man bounding up the steps, two at a time. He was good-looking, with light brown hair, a chiseled face, and chocolate eyes. When he reached them, he swept Claudia into his arms and gave her a big kiss.

"I can see you've already been shopping," Sandro said after Claudia introduced him to Nan-

11

cy, Bess, and George. His English was very good, Nancy noticed. "Beautiful," Sandro said as his eyes came to rest on Bess's necklace. He fingered it appreciatively. "Did you get this at Preziosi?"

"No, Massimo Bianco made it," Bess told him.

Sandro whistled. "Massimo is getting better. He should raise his prices!"

As the five of them talked Nancy learned that Sandro was on his lunch hour from his job for a computer company. "It's good to be outside after being inside all morning," he told the girls.

"It is so beautiful today. We can eat on the steps," Claudia suggested. "Who will come with me to buy some *panini?*"

"Panini?" Bess asked, rummaging in her knapsack for her phrase book. "Is that food?"

"Sandwiches," Claudia explained. "And we will need some *àcqua minerale* to drink."

"Mineral water, right?" George guessed. "I'll go with you, Claudia."

"Well, I'm going to practice my Italian in the piazza," Bess decided. "I saw some earrings down there that I want to get a closer look at. I'll meet you back here, okay?"

Sandro turned to Claudia and briefly spoke to her in Italian. She nodded and said, *"Buon idèa. Sandro will go with you to help, Bess."*

As Sandro and Bess headed down the steps Nancy turned to Claudia. "I guess I'll go with you and George. Now, where can we get those *panini?"*

"I know a great *tavola calda* three blocks away," Claudia told her, starting off down the street at the top of the Spanish Steps. "They have pizza as well."

"Ugh, who could stand anything hot?" George asked, wrinkling her nose. "It's ninety degrees!"

Nancy stopped in her tracks as a loud scream pierced the air. A moment later loud Italian voices and the clatter of running feet echoed off the stone buildings.

"It is coming from the piazza," Claudia said with concern. She, Nancy, and George began to jog back to the steps.

Just as the girls reached the top of the steps, another high-pitched wail rose above the noise. A familiar voice cried, "There they go! Stop them! They have my knapsack!"

"Quick!" George shouted, taking off down the stairs. "It's Bess!"

Chapter

Two

NANCY RACED AFTER GEORGE, with Claudia close behind. At first Nancy couldn't see Bess through the thick knot of people gathered at the foot of the Spanish Steps. As they pushed their way through, she finally spotted Bess sitting on the ground near the fountain. Sandro was kneeling beside her.

"Bess, are you okay?" George asked breathlessly, hurrying over. "Are you hurt?"

There was a shocked expression on Bess's face as she looked up at her friends. "No, I'm fine," she assured everyone, although her voice was a little shaky. Nancy and George quickly helped her to her feet. Seeing that Bess was all right, the crowd of people began to thin out.

"Those awful kids are pickpockets and thieves. They swarm around tourists all the time," Sandro said angrily.

14

"At least your necklace is safe," Claudia commented, seeing the gold beads Bess was clasping tightly in her hand.

Bess blinked as if she had just realized it was there. "Wow, that was intense," she said. "All of a sudden these kids were all around me. They grabbed my knapsack, and the next thing I knew someone pulled at my necklace. They almost got it, too, but then they ran off."

"I guess they got scared," Sandro said. Frowning, he took the necklace from Bess and examined it. "The clasp is broken."

While Bess spoke, Nancy scanned the area. She didn't see any group of kids, but she did spot a splash of aqua next to a trash bin several yards away. "I think I see your knapsack," she told Bess, striding toward the trash bin.

It *was* the knapsack, she saw. As Nancy knelt to collect the scattered contents, Sandro appeared beside her.

"The perfume bottle shattered, but at least everything else will smell good," he said, handing Bess's hotel key and some change to Nancy. "We're in luck. Even her wallet is here."

"But no money," Nancy said, checking it. "At least they didn't take her credit cards." She rummaged inside the knapsack and was relieved to see Bess's passport and traveler's checks, too. "I guess they were just after cash."

"Thanks, guys," Bess said when Nancy and Sandro returned with her things. "To think I bought this knapsack because I thought it would

15

be *better* than carrying around a purse. I feel so silly. Set upon by a gang of little kids!"

"I'm just glad you're not hurt," Nancy said, handing Bess her knapsack. "All your ID is still there, but there's no money in your wallet."

Bess shrugged. "I wasn't carrying much anyway. The guidebooks tell you not to." She stared ruefully at her necklace, which Sandro was still holding. "I feel bad about the broken clasp, though. I mean, Massimo just gave it to me, and I've already broken it."

"I can get it fixed for you," Sandro offered. "My mother knows a good jeweler."

"It might be simpler to take it back to Massimo," Claudia said. With a teasing look at Bess she added, "I bet that will . . . cheer you up—is that the expression?"

Sandro reluctantly handed the necklace to Bess. "At least let me buy you some more perfume. I wasn't very good at protecting you."

"No way," Bess declared, dabbing at her forehead with a tissue she found in her knapsack. "But I will let you talk me into having lunch at a nice air-conditioned restaurant. I think I need to catch my breath!"

"Boy, it's getting hotter by the minute," Bess said an hour later as she, Nancy, George, and Claudia left a small restaurant named Piccolino. Sandro had left a few minutes earlier to return to his job. Now, in the heat of the midday sun, none of the girls felt like walking or getting on a crowded bus to get back to Piazza Navona.

Claudia paused on the sidewalk and looked expectantly at the others. "I have an idea," she said. "Have any of you ever ridden a Vespa?"

"Sure," Nancy replied. "Isn't it like a moped?"

Claudia nodded. "They are a way of life in Rome. Everyone I know has one. Come on, there is a place where we can rent them down the street. We can get you two for the time you are here. You can ride double on the bigger ones."

Under Claudia's direction the girls chose two Vespas and doubled up for the ride. "Just keep your eyes open," Claudia told Nancy and George as she buckled her safety helmet on. "Romans are the worst drivers in the world."

Claudia wasn't kidding, Nancy realized as the fourth driver in a row cut her and George off. George's grip tightened on Nancy as Nancy buzzed around the car in order to keep Claudia and Bess in sight. She was relieved when they reached the piazza and could park the Vespa.

Massimo came bounding over to greet the girls as they approached his jewelry display. "Dancing tonight?" he asked, his dark eyes fixed on Bess.

"Not tonight," Bess said, looking apologetic. "Sandro invited us to dinner at his mother's. But we *are* free tomorrow, right, you guys?" she said, giving Nancy, Claudia, and George a pleading look.

Nancy could see that the others didn't want to stand in the way of Bess's romance, either. "Right," she confirmed. "Dancing sounds great."

"Perfetto. Then it is a date," Massimo said, his smiling eyes trained on Bess.

"Massimo," a low female voice called. Nancy turned and saw a stunning girl with deep green eyes and black hair. She wore a long simple dress splashed with red flowers. She was very petite, only about five feet tall.

"Karine," Massimo said, surprise in his voice. "Um, meet Nancy, Bess, and George. This is Karine Azar. You already know Claudia."

Karine smiled and waved at the girls. Casually she went over and sat on Massimo's stool.

"Azar?" George asked. "Is that Italian?"

"It's Turkish," Karine replied, with a slight lilt in her voice. "But my mother is Italian."

"Karine is an artist, too," Massimo explained. "We go to the same school. She makes chalk drawings in the piazza during the summer." His eyes darted between Bess and Karine, and he looked very uncomfortable. Nancy wondered what the story was between him and Karine.

"What kind of drawings?" Nancy asked Karine, trying to break the tension.

Karine nodded. "Over there." She waved in the direction of a brightly colored drawing on the stone floor of the piazza. It was a depiction of a robed figure.

"That's really great," George commented. "What is it?"

"I usually do one of Rome's great works. Today it is one of the figures from a fresco called *The School of Athens,*" Karine said. "It's supposed to be Aristotle."

After glancing at the drawing Bess took her

necklace out of her knapsack and showed Massimo the broken clasp. "Can you fix it?" she asked.

"*Cèrto*. Of course. Let me get a new clasp and some pliers." Massimo reached for a canvas bag beneath his display table. "This is a beautiful piece," he said as he dug around for supplies. "If I had known you had it, I might even have charged you for the one I gave you this morning."

"What an artist!" Bess teased. "You can't even recognize your own art. This *is* the necklace you gave me this morning."

"No, it is not," Massimo said, wrapping a clear piece of fishing line around the clasp. He tied a knot, pulled it tight, and snipped off the end.

Bess glanced at Nancy and George in confusion. "Of course it's the one you gave me. Why would I buy two necklaces like this?"

Now Massimo was the one who looked confused. "You do not really think this is my necklace," he said. "Did you lose the one I gave you?"

"Massimo gave you a necklace?" Karine spoke up, looking suddenly interested. "And you lost it? If Massimo gave me a necklace, I would never, ever lose it," she declared, catching Massimo's gaze.

Bess had competition, Nancy thought. And Karine was making sure she knew it.

Ignoring Karine, George asked Massimo, "Why do you think that necklace isn't yours?"

"Look at this," he said. He held out a piece of the broken clasp he had just removed. "It is very intricate. My clasps are much simpler. Also, the beads are strung differently. I use fishing line. These beads are knotted onto a braided string."

Massimo fingered the beads carefully. "I am almost certain that these beads are made of real gold."

Bess stared at the necklace in disbelief. "I don't get it. How could this be real gold?"

"It is heavier than my necklaces are, for one thing. And the workmanship is better," Massimo explained. He unhooked one of his necklaces from the velvet board next to him. "See? The beads have seam marks from the mold I make them in. I try to smooth them down, but you can still see marks. These beads do not have that."

Nancy thought back over their day, trying to figure out what could have happened. "Maybe you switched necklaces at Preziosi by accident," she said to Bess. "The one there looked a lot like yours."

"I thought I picked up the right one," Bess said, frowning. "But I guess I could have made a mistake. I was kind of distracted by all the great stuff there."

Claudia shook her head. "There are no real gold necklaces at Preziosi. The jewelry is not *that* precious."

"Are you *sure* it's real gold?" Bess asked again.

"If you do not believe me, ask someone else," Massimo said, looking insulted.

"It's just that"—Bess hesitated briefly—"if it's real gold, it must be worth a lot."

Massimo nodded. "A copy in gold would be worth maybe a few thousand American dollars."

Nancy could hardly believe her ears. How had Bess gotten hold of something so valuable?

Bess, George, and Claudia looked just as shocked as Nancy was. "But it's not from a museum or anything, is it?" Bess asked anxiously.

Massimo shook his head. "If it was, Bess, you would be a very rich woman."

"Well, I'm curious, if nothing else," Nancy said. "Claudia, do you know any jewelry experts who could take a look at this necklace? Unless you want it back, Massimo."

"It is not mine," he said, shaking his head again.

Claudia thought for a moment. "There is Fabio Andreotti," she suggested.

"He is an art dealer," Massimo added.

"He specializes in antiquities," Claudia explained, "so he would probably know what a good copy is worth. I met him at Sandro's house when he was trying to buy Signora Fiorello's jewelry. He is a friend, at least, so he will probably look at it for free."

Massimo nodded. "You know where his office is?"

"I think so," Claudia told him.

Karine had listened to most of the conversation about the necklace without commenting. As the girls got ready to leave she slipped off Massimo's stool. "Come see my drawing the next time you're here," she said. There was a hint of challenge in her green eyes as she glanced at Bess. "When you are not so occupied with Massimo."

The girls drove their Vespas several blocks through the narrow, winding streets behind the piazza, looking for Fabio Andreotti's office. Claudia stopped twice to ask directions in rapid-fire Italian.

Finally they arrived at the old stone building where the office was located. Claudia gave her name to the guard in the lobby, who directed them to the fourth floor. When they got there, a portly woman greeted the girls and asked them to wait. Nancy had been expecting a store or gallery, but they appeared to be in a small office. The receptionist was the only person in sight.

A door on Nancy's left opened, and a man in a double-breasted gray suit and a red-and-yellow tie stepped into the room. He was slender and tall, with a chiseled profile and iron gray hair.

"Claudia Beluggi," he said in Italian, kissing the air near Claudia's cheeks. "Has Signora Fiorello finally decided to take my offer?"

"Not exactly," Claudia replied in English. She introduced Nancy, Bess, and George, then said, "We wondered if you could examine a necklace for us."

Signor Andreotti switched to flawless English. "I have a client coming in fifteen minutes, but I'll see what I can do," he said, glancing at his watch. "Please, come into my office. The light is better there."

The girls followed Signor Andreotti into an

adjoining room. Bess and Claudia sat in two chairs in front of the desk, while Nancy and George settled into a small couch against the wall.

Bess handed over her necklace, and Signor Andreotti turned on a desk lamp, then held the necklace up to the light. Absently he picked up a pair of half-glasses and put them on the bridge of his nose. He gave Claudia a puzzled look, then returned his attention to the necklace.

Squinting, Signor Andreotti twirled one of the beads between his fingers. The girls waited in silence as the art dealer examined every bead.

Finally he put the necklace down and took off his glasses. He turned to Claudia. "Well, my dear, how much do you want?"

Claudia turned to Nancy. "I—" she began.

"I don't want to haggle over money," Signor Andreotti said soothingly. "I'll give you a fair price. How about, ah, twenty-five million lire?"

"Twenty-five million lire!" Bess gasped. "How much is that?"

"About five times as much as this whole trip is costing," George whispered after closing her eyes to think.

Signor Andreotti sighed. "Okay, twenty-six million. But that's my final offer."

Claudia turned to Nancy, a stunned expression on her face. "You know what this means, don't you?" she asked.

"He is saying the necklace is real," Nancy said, nodding slowly. "Bess, this necklace isn't just real gold—it's an authentic Etruscan antiquity!"

Chapter

Three

"OF COURSE IT'S REAL." Signor Andreotti looked from Nancy to Claudia. "Why else would you bring it to me? May I ask whose collection it's from?"

"Well, actually—" Claudia began.

"I think it's fascinating that you can tell so much about a necklace so quickly," Nancy broke in smoothly. "I'd love to know how you do it." She wasn't sure why, but her instincts told her not to mention how they'd gotten the necklace.

Flattered, Signor Andreotti turned to Nancy. "Etruscan jewelry is easier to spot than most—for a professional, that is. Look at the detail of the design. The filigree around the stones is quite fine," he said, touching the center bead. He shifted the necklace, showing Nancy the smaller beads. "See the granulation on these? The Etruscans had a special way of working with gold. It's a lost art."

"Wow," Bess said, her blue eyes wide.

Signor Andreotti gave her a brief smile and turned back to the necklace. "The gold beads aren't perfect. When you roll them slightly you can tell they aren't absolutely round. That means they were made by hand, not machine."

He handed Bess the necklace. "There's no doubt in my mind that this necklace is authentic."

"Thank you," Claudia said. "I am sorry we took so much of your time. I promise we will bring the necklace back if we decide to sell it."

As the girls headed for the door, Signor Andreotti stopped them. "Claudia, this may be presumptuous, but since you won't tell me who the necklace belongs to, you and your friends might want to know one thing. You would have a very hard time taking it out of the country. It's an antiquity, after all."

"I don't understand," George said. "Does it belong to the government?"

"That depends," the art dealer replied. "There are some pieces in the hands of wealthy families and certain dealers. But for the most part, it is illegal to remove ancient artifacts from the country."

The four girls thanked Signor Andreotti again and left. A wave of heat hit them when they got out to the street.

"I don't get it. A real Etruscan necklace doesn't just show up out of nowhere," Nancy finally said. "Claudia, are you sure it couldn't have come from Preziosi?"

"Positive." Claudia nodded. "All the necklaces

at the store are fakes. Massimo makes them. And I know the package I opened was from him because Sandro dropped it off and gave it directly to me. It was still sealed shut today when I found it in the back."

"If the necklace didn't come from Preziosi, that brings us back to Massimo," George put in.

Bess gave Claudia a questioning look. "Why would Sandro drop off a package for Massimo?"

"The computer store where he works is not far from Piazza Navona," Claudia explained. "Massimo cannot always come to the store when he is busy. Since Sandro is my boyfriend, he brings necklaces here from Massimo when he visits me."

Nancy sighed. None of this was making any sense. Unless . . .

"I hate to say it, but we may have stumbled onto a theft," she said soberly. "After what Signor Andreotti just told us, it seems pretty obvious that these necklaces are very valuable and difficult to come by."

"Something tells me that Massimo is the key to figuring out where this necklace came from," George added. "On the other hand, he didn't seem to be familiar with it, either."

"Do you think someone would hide a real necklace with Massimo's fakes?" Bess asked. "That seems awfully risky."

Nancy gave her friends a meaningful look. "It's less risky if Massimo knows about it."

"But if he knew, he would have taken the necklace back," Bess protested. "We offered it to him."

26

She was right, Nancy realized. "Well, it had to come from him or the store," she said. "Claudia, do you think Preziosi's owner might know anything about the necklace?"

Claudia made an empty-handed gesture. "Perhaps. Paola Rinzini owns the store, but she is visiting a supplier today. And Preziosi is closed tomorrow. She should be around on Monday, though. Can you wait until then?"

"I guess we'll have to," Nancy said. "In the meantime, let's see if the necklace has been reported stolen. If it has, we can return it. Then we won't have to worry about having something so expensive on our hands."

"Let me see if I can find someone who can help us," Claudia said as the girls headed up the broad stairs of the police station and entered a quiet lobby. "We need someone simpatico."

Looking around, Nancy noticed that several officers in dark blue uniforms with flat hats were milling around. Others escorted nonuniformed people down a long hall.

"All these officers look pretty sympathetic to me," Bess commented, noticing several male heads turn their way.

"*Simpatico* means nice or helpful," George said, rolling her eyes.

The two cousins and Nancy waited on a bench near the entrance while Claudia approached the main desk and spoke with the officer there.

A few minutes later Claudia returned with an attractive young officer whose badge read Gianni

27

Franchi. Officer Franchi ushered them down a side hall and into an office where an older police officer was waiting.

Claudia spoke Italian. Nancy had almost no trouble understanding as Claudia gave the two men a brief account of their day, saying that they had bought the necklace from a street vendor. When the clasp broke, they took it to a jeweler, who thought the necklace might be real. Claudia finished by saying that she wondered if there were any reports of a robbery, because she wanted to make sure the necklace wasn't connected to any kind of crime.

The older officer spoke briefly to Claudia, then got up and left the office. "No thefts have been reported here," Claudia explained to Nancy, Bess, and George. "He's going to see if there are any reports from the carabinieri—that's the national police."

At Officer Franchi's request Bess brought out the necklace. He snapped a few pictures with an instant camera. He, too, spoke in Italian, but again, Nancy was able to understand what he said.

"We can make some discreet inquiries," the officer told Claudia. "And we'll check with some of the museums. Will you leave the necklace here?"

Nancy spoke up quickly, trying out her Italian. She told Officer Franchi that she would rather keep the necklace, if it wasn't stolen. "After all, we did buy it," she finished.

Officer Franchi's heavy eyebrows drew together. He gave her a calculating stare, then spoke again to

Claudia. Obviously he didn't like Nancy's idea, even after Claudia assured him that Nancy was a detective. But Nancy didn't think he had the right to take the necklace from them, either.

Officer Franchi broke off as his partner returned. Shrugging his shoulders, the older officer reported that there were no thefts that the carabinieri knew of.

Before the girls left, the police officers took Claudia's name and address, as well as passport numbers from Nancy, Bess, and George. As an afterthought, Nancy wrote down the name and phone number of the chief of police back in River Heights, the girls' hometown. "Perhaps you could use some kind of reference," she told Officer Franchi. She knew how much Chief McGinnis respected her. Perhaps talking to him would help Officer Franchi to trust her more.

"What was that all about?" George asked Nancy and Claudia as the girls left the building. "I didn't understand much, but it didn't exactly look like you made a best friend in there."

Nancy filled in the details of the meeting for Bess and George. Claudia let out a sigh when Nancy was done. "Officer Franchi doesn't trust us, that's for sure," she added.

"So we're back to square one. We have no idea where this necklace came from," Bess said. "How are we going to keep it safe?"

As the girls reached the bottom of the steps outside the police station, Claudia bent down to unlock the Vespa she and Bess had been riding. "Bring it to Sandro's tonight," she suggested. "His mother has a large collection of jewelry that she keeps in a safe. I am sure she would hold it for you if you asked her."

"Great," said Bess, looking relieved. "I'll definitely talk to her."

Sandro and his mother lived in a magnificent old building called the Theater of Marcellus. When Claudia had given the girls directions, she told them it had been built in ancient times by two emperors, Julius Caesar and Caesar Augustus.

"It looks like a small version of the Colosseum," Nancy called out to Bess and George as they drove up on their Vespas. She pointed out the two rows of crumbling archways in the front of the building. The girls rode up the ramp to the back of the building, where they parked. Then they walked into the lobby.

"It's like a ruin on the outside, but look at the inside!" Bess said in awe.

The lobby was impressive, Nancy had to agree. The floors were made of beautiful inlaid marble in intricate geometric patterns. The high ceilings were painted with flying cherubs.

"Maybe we should have dressed up more for dinner," George said, smoothing the skirt of her red cotton sundress.

Nancy looked down at her jeans skirt and flowered blouse, then at Bess's white pantsuit. "I'm sure Claudia would have told us if we should."

A pleasant doorman announced their arrival

over the intercom, and the girls stepped into the wrought-iron cage elevator. Claudia had said the Fiorellos lived on the top floor, so Nancy pressed the button. With a rattle they eased upward.

The elevator opened directly into a large, airy apartment. The living room was visible just beyond the foyer, and Nancy saw Claudia sitting on an elegant leather couch. She was talking to a half-dozen other young people who were scattered around the room.

Seeing the girls, Claudia hurried over to greet them. Sandro was right behind her.

"Buòna séra," he said, kissing each girl on both cheeks. "I'm so happy you could come meet our friends."

Within seconds Nancy, Bess, and George were laughing and gesturing with the others as they all tried to make themselves understood.

"Originally we were just having dinner," Sandro told Nancy, his arm resting on Claudia's shoulder. "Then we found out Domenico and his friends are leaving tomorrow to climb Mount Olympus or something, so we invited everyone over so we could say farewell. Then when you came, we invited you so we could say welcome!"

George's brown eyes gleamed with interest. She turned to an Italian girl with short, spiky hair, whom Sandro had introduced as Daniela. "You guys are climbing Mount Olympus?" George asked.

"Actually, they're going to Greece to visit the site of the ancient Olympics," Claudia told her.

31

"What a great thing to do!" George exclaimed. "You know, our next stop is Greece. Maybe we'll do that, too."

Bess looked horrified. "Over my dead body," she told her cousin firmly. "We did enough mountain climbing when we were in the Alps."

Despite Bess's veto, Nancy could tell that George was very excited about the idea. As Daniela and a blond-haired guy named Domenico told George all about their planned trip, she listened eagerly.

Signora Fiorello didn't appear in the living room until dinner was almost ready. Sandro introduced the girls to his mother as all of the teenagers got up to help put the food on the table. Nancy immediately liked the robust, gray-haired woman. She was the picture of an adoring mother.

All through the pasta, the veal entrée, and the salad, Signora Fiorello kept up a steady stream of conversation about Sandro. George was at the other end of the table, still talking to Domenico and Daniela, so Nancy and Bess got the full force of Signora Fiorello's doting.

"Oh, yes, he is really quite an electronic genius," she said, speaking to Nancy and Bess in very good English. "The shop where he works as a computer consultant would be lost without him." She smiled proudly at Sandro, who was seated next to her. "Of course, after a few years there he could go out on his own, maybe even open his own company. But first he must get more experience."

Sandro looked completely embarrassed by his

mother's rambling. "I have plenty of experience," he objected. "I could be a big success now."

Claudia bent close to Nancy. "I have heard this same argument a million times," she said. "Sandro is very frustrated not to be working for himself."

Nancy nodded her understanding, feeling thankful that her own father was so supportive of everything she did.

"You young people are so eager to grow up," Signora Fiorello said. She took Sandro's hand and patted it affectionately, not appearing to notice his grimace. "Are you in school?" she asked Nancy.

"Not right now," Nancy replied.

"So what is it you do, if I may ask?"

"Well, occasionally I help my father or his friends do some investigating. He's a lawyer," Nancy said, trying to avoid the topic. What would Signora Fiorello think of some of the scrapes she had gotten herself into during her cases!

"See?" Signora Fiorello said triumphantly to Sandro. "She helps her father and his friends. She is not trying to start a business so young."

Sandro rolled his eyes, not bothering to hide his frustration. For the rest of the meal he ignored his mother, devoting his attention to his food.

When dinner was finished the girls lingered in the living room after Domenico and his friends left. Claudia told Sandro's mother about their day and about Bess's necklace. When she got to the part about Signor Andreotti's belief that the necklace was authentic, Sandro whistled.

33

"You didn't tell me that," he said. "He must be mistaken. Massimo wouldn't have a real necklace."

"I hope you have it in a safe place, my dear," Signora Fiorello told Bess. "Fabio Andreotti is a good friend and an excellent art dealer. If he says it is real, it is real."

Bess looked at Claudia, who nodded slightly. "Actually, I have the necklace in my knapsack," Bess said. She drew it out and held it up to the light. "I'm not really sure what to do with it. It's so valuable that I feel nervous about carrying it around."

"I have a safe," Sandro's mother offered immediately, leaning forward to look at the necklace. "You could leave it with me."

"That's a great idea," Sandro agreed. "Then we'd be sure it's secure."

George smiled and said, "Actually, Claudia mentioned that you have a safe. Are you sure you wouldn't mind?"

"Of course not. Come with me," Signora Fiorello said immediately. "I will show you my own Etruscan necklace, and then we will put yours safely away."

"Mamma," Sandro said, "they don't want to see your jewelry."

"Oh, I'd love to," Bess protested.

Signora Fiorello beamed at Bess and took her arm. She led the way down the hall to a large, feminine bedroom and went over to the wall next to her desk. A large painting hung there. With

Sandro's help she removed it and set it on the floor. Behind the painting was a wall safe.

Nancy and her friends kept a tactful distance while Signora Fiorello spun the combination. All the while she chatted about her own jewelry collection. Sandro rolled his eyes, his face red. His mother's banter was obviously embarrassing him.

"Here we go," Signora Fiorello said as the safe door swung open. She moved a few things around, frowning as she looked into the safe.

"Where did I put them?" she said, a note of panic creeping into her voice. "The box was right on top."

She started taking boxes out and putting them on her desk. Finally everything was on the desk, and the safe stood empty. After checking each box Signora Fiorello looked disbelievingly at the empty safe.

"It's gone," she said in a strangled voice. "My Etruscan necklace is gone!"

Chapter

Four

"CALL THE POLICE," Sandro said to Claudia, his face pale. Hurrying over to his mother, he led her to the bed, and she lay down. Signora Fiorello wore a look of utter shock.

As Claudia picked up the telephone on the desk, Nancy went over to the safe. Carefully using one fingernail, she swung the door toward her by its edge, then examined the area by the lock.

"No sign of a forced entry," she reported to Bess and George, who were hovering behind her. "At least none that I can see. Maybe the police can come up with a set of fingerprints."

"They are on their way," Claudia said as she replaced the telephone receiver in its cradle.

While they waited for the police Nancy, George, and Bess stood at the far end of the room and talked quietly about the upsetting event. Nancy gestured to the pile of boxes on the desk. "There's still a lot of jewelry here," she said to her friends in a low tone. "A professional thief wouldn't leave all this behind. I wonder if she could have misplaced the necklace." At the moment, however, she didn't think she should question Signora Fiorello. She was too upset.

Sandro, who had left the room, returned holding a damp towel. As he was placing the towel on his mother's forehead the doorbell buzzed. "Claudia, can you get that?" Sandro asked.

Claudia left the bedroom, returning a moment later with two policemen. Nancy hung back and watched as the officers checked the safe and dusted for prints. They asked Sandro for a list of the missing items.

"I'm not sure what was in the safe," Sandro said. He tightened his arm around his mother. "Mamma, could you take another look?"

After she spent some time going through her belongings, Signora Fiorello reported that only the necklace was gone. She rummaged in her desk drawer and eventually pulled out a photograph. "I have this for the insurance company," she said, holding up a picture of a heavy gold choker with ornate gold flowers and scarabs hanging from it.

The police took the photograph for evidence, promising to return it. After asking a few more questions they left.

Signora Fiorello seemed to have recovered herself, Nancy saw. "I have some delicious peach iced tea in the kitchen," she told the teenagers. "I think we could all use something refreshing." Turning to Bess, she added, "Obviously your necklace will not be safe with me. You had better keep it yourself."

When the group was settled at a round table in the kitchen, Signora Fiorello turned to Nancy. "Claudia says you are a detective," she said. "Is that what you do for your father and his friends?"

When Nancy nodded, she continued. "Would you do it for me? Find out who took my necklace?"

"I can try," Nancy said. The truth was, she was dying to investigate and had already been thinking over the crime. "I think maybe Bess's necklace and yours are connected somehow."

A panicked look came over Signora Fiorello. "A serial crime? Oh, no! I must call Renata and warn her. And Alessa." She turned to Sandro and asked, "She has Etruscan jewelry, right?"

"Mamma!" Sandro objected. "How would I know?"

Signora Fiorello picked up the telephone. When she finally put it down ten minutes later, she had astounding news. She had asked her friends to check their own jewelry, and both of them were also missing their Etruscan pieces!

"The police are going to have a busy night," Nancy said grimly. "Did they say anything else?" she asked Sandro's mother.

Only Etruscan jewelry had been stolen, Nancy discovered, even though Signora Fiorello's friends had other valuables, too. None of the missing necklaces matched the one Bess had. Sandro's mother then called two other acquaintances who had Etruscan jewelry and learned they were on vacation. Bess's necklace might have been stolen from one of them.

After promising to look into the thefts the next day Nancy, Bess, and George said a weary good night. As they left the Theater of Marcellus, George said, "Well, Nan, it looks like we're getting more than we bargained for on this trip!"

Nancy groaned, tugging on the outside door of the building where Pensione Antonio was located. "I forgot that they said they lock this place up at night," she said. "Does anyone have a key?"

George pulled a ring of keys from her bag and unlocked the door. The girls entered the plain stone lobby of the building and walked up the curving staircase to the second floor. The door to the pensione was at the top of the stairs. Going quietly inside, they made their way down the hall to their room.

"Are you guys really tired?" George asked, sitting on the edge of one of the three beds.

Nancy could tell something was on her friend's mind. George had remained quiet and thoughtful for most of the evening, even before Sandro's mother had discovered her necklace was gone. Apparently Bess had noticed it, too.

"Do you want to talk?" Bess asked, dropping into the room's only chair.

Nancy sat on the bed next to George and hugged

her. "It's about Greece, isn't it?" she guessed. "You're dying to go with Sandro's friends on that trip, right?"

George nodded. "It *is* our next stop, and Daniela said I could room with her," she said. "I could meet you guys in Athens. Unless you don't want to go there anymore," she added quickly.

"I thought Domenico and the group were leaving tomorrow morning," Bess said. "How are you going to get hold of them?"

George smiled sheepishly. "Domenico said if I decided to come, I could meet them at the train station in the morning. They're taking a train to the ferry."

"Well, before I give you my permission, just tell me this," Bess said, pretending to be stern. "Is it really the trip to Greece you're dying for, or is it Domenico?"

George rolled her eyes. "Bess, just because you have a guy in every country doesn't mean I want that," she said with a teasing grin. "Besides," she added, pulling a packet of letters from the front pocket of her shoulder bag, "I miss Kevin too much to think about dating other guys."

Kevin Davis, George's boyfriend, was a sports announcer back in the States. Nancy knew how serious George was about their relationship. She definitely wasn't the type to go chasing another guy all over Europe.

Nancy sighed as she thought of the three letters she had received from her own boyfriend, Ned Nickerson. He really missed her, but so far she'd written him only one postcard, from the Italian

Riviera. She kept telling herself she'd write a long letter—tomorrow—but somehow the time was never right. She hadn't admitted it even to Bess and George, but the truth was, she thought more about Mick Devlin these days than about the boy who had been her one and only love for a long, long time.

Pushing aside her disturbing thoughts, Nancy leaned over and hugged George. "Go ahead to Greece," she told her. "I'm sure seeing Mount Olympus will be great. And we'll fill you in on everything that happens here."

"Sure," Bess agreed. "We were planning to be in Athens next Saturday anyway. We can just meet at that hotel where we made reservations. In case there's any change of plans, though, why don't you call here and leave a message with the number of where you'll be staying with Daniela?"

"That's a good idea," George said. She gave Nancy a probing look. "Are you sure you're not upset about this?" she asked. "I mean, if you need my help investigating those necklaces . . ."

"We'll be fine," Nancy and Bess said at once.

Grinning at her friends, George said. "Thanks, guys. You're the best!"

"You have to fill me in on some of this, Nan," Bess pleaded early the next afternoon. "I didn't understand half the words! I was going to pull out my phrase book, but I was too embarrassed."

After seeing George off with Daniela and the others at the train station, Bess and Nancy had visited the two friends of Signora Fiorello who

41

had also had Etruscan jewelry stolen. Now they were sitting down to pasta at a small, family-run restaurant near the Forum.

"Well, neither of their houses looked as if it had been broken into," Nancy said. "And both have alarm systems that weren't triggered. Neither woman had been away for any length of time, either; their vacations are scheduled for August."

"I understood what Signora Bellini said about everybody knowing they have the jewelry, thanks to the paparazzi," Bess put in, referring to the photographers that swarmed around the social events where the women often wore their jewelry.

Just then the waiter brought steaming plates of pasta to the table and set them down.

Bess picked up her fork with relish. "This is fantastic!" she said, smacking her lips. "I love this spicy sauce. What do they call it again?"

"Arrabbiata," Nancy said. "Mine is great, too."

Bess speared some of the short, tubular pasta with her fork, then popped it into her mouth. "I didn't understand what Signora Bellini said about Fabio Andreotti, though," she said, getting back to the case. "And Signora Cresci mentioned him, too, right?"

Nancy nodded. "I asked if anyone had shown a special interest in the jewelry, and they both mentioned Andreotti," she told Bess. "Signora Bellini said that he has offered to buy her necklace so many times that it's become a formality—part joke and part compliment."

"Do you think he wanted their jewelry badly enough to steal it?" Bess looked doubtful. "He seemed so nice."

"I don't know," Nancy admitted. "Most of the people we've met think the world of him, including Sandro's mother. But I think we should find out more about him."

"Would you believe I think I'm going to fall asleep?" Bess declared as the girls left the restaurant a short while later. "Didn't Claudia say there's an Italian tradition about napping after lunch?"

"Yesterday was a long day," Nancy said. "And we're going dancing tonight, remember?"

"That's right! I can't possibly fall asleep at the disco. I'd die of embarrassment."

"All right." Nancy laughed. "A siesta it is." The girls chugged down the streets on their Vespas to their pensione. After locking the Vespas they entered the building. The lobby felt cool and slightly damp as they walked in. Their footsteps echoed as they went up the stairs.

When they reached the second floor the family that ran the pensione was nowhere in sight. The front desk of the hotel was empty.

"Maybe we could check out Fabio Andreotti later this afternoon," Nancy suggested as they walked down the hall to their room.

"Sure," Bess said, putting her key in the lock and pushing open the door. She stepped forward and stopped, staring inside.

43

"Nancy?" she asked in a small voice.

"Hmm?" Nancy looked over Bess's shoulder— and gasped.

Bess's bed was overturned. Clothes and belongings were strewn across the floor and furniture. The room had been ransacked!

Chapter

Five

I T'S THE NECKLACE," Bess whispered in a horrified voice. "The thief is after us!"

"Maybe not," Nancy said, although she suspected Bess was right. "See if you can find out what's missing, but don't move anything. I'll get help."

Nancy ran down the hall to the front desk and rang the bell. A few minutes later the young woman who managed the pensione poked her head sleepily from behind a curtained door. She had curly, dark hair and a round face. Seeing Nancy, she stepped out to the desk.

"Signora Verona," Nancy said, remembering the woman's name from when the girls checked in. Quickly she explained what had happened and led Signora Verona back to the room.

"I don't think anything was stolen," Bess said, straightening up. "But the room's a mess."

Nancy nodded, then turned to Signora Verona. "Did anyone come in looking for us?" she asked, speaking in Italian. "Did you see anyone acting suspiciously?"

The woman shook her head. "No. Only our guests. I didn't see anyone else."

"But you weren't at the desk when we came in," Nancy pointed out gently. "Maybe someone got in without your seeing them."

"The front door is locked at night and when we aren't on duty," Signora Verona replied. "Every guest has a key, so I don't always look out when I hear the door."

Nancy frowned. The outside door had been ajar when she and Bess had come in just now, she remembered. It could have been that way all afternoon. If not, anyone with a key to the pensione door could have broken into Bess's room.

"Could someone have seen our room number?" Nancy asked.

The woman shook her head vigorously. "My rooming list is in the back with me," she said. "No one came in there. I'd better call the police," she continued.

Nancy remembered how unhelpful the police had been. "Would you mind if we talked to some of the other guests ourselves instead?" she asked. She would probably get more information that way.

The young woman pressed her lips together. "I will talk to the guests," she finally decided. "But if any other rooms were disturbed, I will have to call the police."

After Signora Verona left, Nancy helped Bess get her mattress back on the bed frame. "Who knows our room number?" Nancy asked, thinking out loud. "Did you tell Massimo or Claudia?"

Bess shook her head. "I didn't tell anyone. I barely know what the room number is myself!"

"Well, if other rooms were hit, we'll know soon enough," Nancy said. "If not, it looks as if the necklace really *was* the target."

"So someone knows I have this real Etruscan necklace," Bess said anxiously. "And whoever it is must be a criminal to tear our room up like this to try to get it." Nodding toward her knapsack, she added, "Carrying this necklace around is really making me nervous, Nan."

This case was definitely starting to heat up, Nancy had to agree. "I'll keep it in my shoulder bag from now on, if you like," she offered. "Meanwhile, let's go ask Signora Verona if anyone saw anything."

The girls found the pensione manager at the front desk. The other guests were mostly young students on vacation, Signora Verona told Nancy. None of them remembered seeing or hearing anything suspicious, and none of the other rooms in the pensione had been disturbed.

After Signora Verona retreated into the back room, Bess flopped down onto a chair next to the lobby desk. "Now what?" she asked Nancy. "I mean, that proves that the break-in is directly tied to the necklace, right?"

"I'd like to talk to Paola Rinzini, the owner of

Preziosi," Nancy said. "Maybe she knows where
the real necklace came from."

"But Claudia told us the store's closed today,"
Bess said, frowning.

Nancy walked over to the pay phone next to the
pensione door. She took some Italian coins out of
her pocket. "Oh, I forgot!" she exclaimed. "This
phone only takes those special coins, *gettóni.*"
When they had called Claudia on Friday night,
Signora Verona had sold them one of the phone
tokens. "I'd better buy a few of them," Nancy
said. "We're probably going to need them."

The girls called out to Signora Verona again,
and she sold them some *gettóni.* Then they called
Claudia and got Paola Rinzini's home telephone
number.

"Paola's not home," Nancy said, hanging up the
phone after trying the woman's number. "We'll
have to wait until tomorrow, I guess." There was a
determined glint in her eyes as she added, "But
I'm going to keep my eye on Massimo while we're
dancing tonight."

Nancy and Bess had arranged to meet Claudia,
Sandro, and Massimo at a club in Trastevere, a
neighborhood filled with colorful nightspots. As
the pounding beat of the music bounced off the
ceiling and came down around them, Nancy tried
to spot their friends through the whirling crowd on
the dance floor.

"I don't see them," she said, leading the way to
the bar. "Let's get some sodas."

Bess grimaced as she spotted a familiar face at one of the tables. "It's Karine," she moaned. "I hope Massimo didn't ask her to come here, too."

Just then the crowd surged around them, and Massimo stepped out of it. "You both look fantastic!" he said loudly, fighting to be heard over the music. "Are you ready to dance for your necklace?" he asked Bess.

"I'll dance all night," Bess replied, giving him a flirtatious look. From where she was standing Nancy had a clear view of Karine Azar. The girl was looking right at them.

"Before we do, let's tell Claudia and Sandro that you are here," Massimo said. He lightly touched Bess's back as he guided the girls around the dance floor. "They have a table for us."

If Massimo knew Karine was there, he was ignoring her, Nancy decided as she watched the sparks fly again between him and Bess.

Claudia and Sandro were whispering, heads together, when Massimo and the girls approached. "So what did you do today?" Claudia asked, pulling herself away from Sandro as Nancy and Bess settled themselves at the table.

Nancy and Bess quickly told the others about their room being ransacked, and the three Italians chorused their alarm.

"You should move to my house," Claudia said firmly when Nancy and Bess finished talking. "You cannot stay in that dangerous place."

"I'd rather have someplace to put our valuables, including this necklace," Nancy said, patting her

49

purse discreetly. "Until I do, I'm not going to let this bag out of my sight."

"Well, Sandro's safe was not a good place," Claudia said, tossing her long black hair over her shoulder. "And my family does not have one. I want to help you, but there is no place I would trust. Unless you want to go back to the police?"

"Things can disappear there as well," Sandro warned. "Evidence sometimes gets misplaced at the police station, especially if it's expensive."

Standing up, he offered, "Can I get anyone a soda?" After taking everyone's order, he headed off for the bar, the multicolored lights playing over his light brown hair.

"Have you figured out where the necklace came from yet?" Massimo asked Bess. "And what you did with the one I gave you?"

"Massimo," Claudia said, "that necklace *must* be from you! If it is not the one you gave Bess at the stand, then she accidentally switched it with one from the last package you sent to Preziosi."

Massimo looked at Claudia. "What package? I didn't send any package over."

"Yes you did. You gave it to Sandro the other day." Claudia's dark eyes flashed impatiently.

"The other day," Massimo said slowly, raking his hand through his wavy black hair. "Oh, I know what you mean. The other week is more like it."

"Stop fooling around!" Claudia demanded, her voice sharp. "When did you give it to him?"

Massimo jumped to his feet, looking insulted. "Everything is so suspicious for you!" he said angrily. "If you want to give me credit for giving Bess an expensive necklace, fine. She is certainly worth it! Come on, Bess, dance with me."

Nancy watched Bess and Massimo move onto the floor. She had to admit they made a handsome couple. If only she could be sure he had nothing to do with the jewelry thefts. But his evasions and denials certainly seemed suspicious.

Sandro returned with the soft drinks a moment later, breaking into Nancy's thoughts. Seeing that Bess and Massimo were on the dance floor, he invited Nancy to dance. She moved easily to the music, but she couldn't keep her mind from dwelling on the missing jewelry. After the first song she signaled that she wanted to sit down.

"Sandro," Claudia asked when he and Nancy had returned, "do you remember that package of necklaces you brought to the store for Massimo? When was that, two days ago now?"

Sandro nodded.

"When did he give them to you?" Claudia's voice was casual, but her eyes stared intensely.

"I'm not sure, um . . ." Sandro narrowed his eyes as he thought. "It was a couple of days before that, maybe more." He gave the girls a sheepish look. "I didn't exactly hurry over with it. I was busy at work."

Great, Nancy thought dejectedly. Sandro was only adding to the confusion. Was there a reason Claudia couldn't get a straight answer out of either guy?

The music picked up again. Bess returned to the table alone as Sandro and Claudia got up to dance.

51

"What a hunk!" Bess said, following Massimo's broad shoulders with her eyes. He had stopped to talk to some friends at a nearby table.

"Now that you've let him go, Karine may grab him for a dance. She was really staring at the two of you when we came in," Nancy said, nodding toward the table where Karine and her friends sat.

Bess shrugged. "Massimo told me all about her. He had a crush on Karine for years, but she just wanted to be friends. Now I guess she's regretting her decision."

"So it's official between you two, then?" Nancy asked, her eyes gleaming. "Is it love?"

Bess seemed to consider Nancy's question for a moment. "You know, I don't think so," she finally said, taking a sip of her soda. "I mean, he's gorgeous, but there's something missing."

Nancy stared at Bess in surprise. "But you two look crazy about each other."

"Sure, we flirt, but somehow it feels more like we're just friends," Bess said. "I know it doesn't sound like me at all," she added, giggling. "Maybe he's just not my type."

"Not your type? Is Bess Marvin turning her back on romance?" Nancy looked around in mock panic. "Quick, someone get a doctor!"

"Is that so surprising?" Bess asked. "I mean, you're always turning down romance. Just look at Mick. I know you liked him, but you just said ciao and took off for Rome."

Nancy fell silent, remembering their time in Geneva. "I didn't know where the relationship would go," she said softly. "I couldn't ask him to come with us because, well, that would have meant too much, too fast. I guess I didn't want to make a decision, so I let the train make it for me."

After a moment Bess asked softly, "What about Ned?"

Nancy sighed. "That's the million-dollar question," she said ruefully. "I only wish I knew how I felt about him."

She looked up as a guy with dark hair and bright blue eyes asked her to dance. "Sure," she decided. Anything to stop thinking about her confused love life. A stream of cute guys swept her into one dance after another, and Nancy didn't have a second to think about Ned or Mick or the stolen Etruscan necklaces.

At about midnight she found herself dancing with Massimo. In the middle of a long medley of songs she began feeling drowsy. At first she thought she was tired because it was so late. She tried gamely to keep dancing with the beat, but her arms began to feel heavy.

"Nancy, are you okay?" Massimo asked, noticing her distress. He helped her back to the table.

The room was spinning even after Nancy sat down. She looked for Bess, Sandro, and Claudia but didn't see any of them among the dancers. Resting her head on the table, she tried breathing deeply.

Massimo put his arm gently around her shoulders. "You do not look well," he said. "Let me take you home."

"I hate to ruin everyone's evening," Nancy said weakly. Strange tingling sensations began crawling up her legs. Her body, which had felt so heavy a moment ago, now seemed very light.

"Come on, we should go," Massimo said, grabbing Nancy's purse and raising her to her feet.

"The bathroom," Nancy said, bracing herself on the table with her hands. "Let me splash some water on my face. Where's my shoulder bag?"

Massimo handed it to her. "I really think we should leave instead."

Nancy gritted her teeth and headed for the bathroom. She wove unsteadily, stumbling a few times as bobbing dancers bumped into her. Dizziness hit her in waves.

This is not exhaustion, Nancy said to herself as she fought to make it to the bathroom. Just inside the door she felt the floor pitch beneath her. Helplessly, Nancy looked around, unable to call out. With a little moan she felt herself falling as blackness closed in around her.

Chapter

Six

"NANCY!" Bess's worried voice reached into the inky dizziness in Nancy's mind. "What happened?"

Nancy forced her eyes open. She was lying on the bathroom floor, her head on Bess's lap.

"I can't . . ." Nancy began weakly, trying to say she couldn't move. The words wouldn't come.

"Shush," Bess said. "You're lucky I was here. I'll go get some help."

Nancy closed her eyes as she felt Bess slip away. I've been drugged, she told herself. Was someone trying to get to the necklace? If so, the thief was definitely among their little group. They were the only ones who knew she had it.

Bess was returning with Massimo. Nancy tried to warn Bess to watch her bag, but Bess told her not to speak. Nancy was dimly aware of Massimo picking her up and carrying her out of the club.

"We will go to the hospital," he told Bess as he placed Nancy gently in a cab a minute later.

"No!" Nancy managed to croak out. She'd lose her bag in a minute at a hospital.

"Why don't you take us back to the pensione?" Bess suggested. "If you help me get her to the room, I'm sure she'll be okay in the morning."

Good job, Bess, Nancy thought. The cab doors slammed closed, and Nancy felt Bess gently move a strand of hair off her face. Then she went spiraling back into unconsciousness.

When Nancy woke Monday morning, sunlight was streaming through the window. Her head ached as she looked around the room.

Bess was perched on the edge of her bed. Seeing that Nancy was awake, she jumped up. "I've been so worried about you!" she exclaimed.

Nancy tested her voice. "I was drugged." Looking around, she saw her bag on the dresser.

"Don't worry, the necklace is in there," Bess said, following Nancy's gaze. "You were holding on to it with a death grip. I had to pry it out of your hands once we got back to the room."

Nancy smiled weakly. "I think someone was after it, and that's why I was drugged."

"Who?" Bess asked, pouring water from a large bottle of mineral water they had bought the day before. She gave it to Nancy.

"Maybe you can help me figure it out. Mmm, this is good," she said as the water soothed her dry throat.

"You need some food," Bess told her. "I'll go out and get some." She started for the door, but Nancy stopped her.

She swung her legs to the floor and stretched her arms. "I need a shower, and I need to get out of here," Nancy said. "Give me a few minutes, and we'll have breakfast at that café down the street."

Twenty minutes later the girls were seated at the café with *caffè latte,* fresh fruit, and pastries on the table in front of them.

"I was redoing my makeup when you came staggering into the ladies' room," Bess said, picking up a pastry. "You were so out of it you didn't even notice me. You really scared Massimo, too. He was hovering by the door when I came out."

"Where were Sandro and Claudia?"

"Massimo said he looked for them, but they weren't around. He was going back to the club to find them after he left us. You don't think one of them . . ." Bess's voice trailed off.

"I don't know, but it certainly seems funny that they disappeared," Nancy said. She toyed with the fruit on her plate. "And I did tell Claudia I had the necklace in my bag."

Bess looked up in surprise. "That's right. When we were talking about the break-in," she remembered. "Everyone was there, come to think of it. You said you weren't going to let the necklace out of your sight." She frowned and added, "You don't think Claudia's mixed up in this, do you?"

"Maybe not," Nancy admitted, trying to piece together her thoughts. "If Claudia wanted the necklace, she could have offered to safeguard it last night and then just taken it. But she didn't do that."

Bess nodded. "What about Sandro?" she asked.

"I've been wondering about him, too," Nancy admitted. "He acted weird when Claudia tried to figure out when he gave her those necklaces. But on the other hand, he doesn't show much interest in jewelry. Massimo's the one who knows about it."

A disconsolate look came into Bess's eyes as she took another bite of her pastry. "Massimo's still the top suspect, isn't he?" she asked. "He was with you when you started feeling sick. So maybe he put something in your drink and stayed with you so he could get into your bag."

"Maybe," Nancy agreed. "At this point, we have to consider everyone. The only suspect we have who couldn't have drugged me is Fabio Andreotti."

Bess crinkled her nose in distaste. "Why does it have to be one of our friends? Maybe the thief was in the crowd at the club and overheard what you said. Maybe it was Karine!"

"I don't know," Nancy said, taking another sip of *caffè latte*. "I think we would have noticed if she was lurking around."

"A friend of Karine's, then. Someone from that group whom we don't know."

Nancy still wasn't convinced. "Well, I think we should find out a little more about our friends before we go after strangers."

"How are we going to find out?"

Stirring her coffee with her spoon, Nancy thought for a moment. "I think we should find out where Massimo lives and drop by his apartment when he's not there. If he's the thief, maybe the other stolen necklaces are there," she said. "But first I want to talk to the owner of Preziosi. Let's call Claudia and set up our day."

The girls returned to their pensione and used the phone by the front desk to call Preziosi. Claudia answered. "Massimo said you fainted at the club," she said as soon as she found out who was calling. "Are you okay?"

"I'm fine," Nancy assured her. "I'm sorry we left without letting you know. Were you still there? We couldn't find you or Sandro."

"I am sorry. We looked all over for you. Massimo said you refused to see a doctor. Are you sure? We have a very good family doctor."

"Really, it was nothing," Nancy repeated. She couldn't help wondering if Claudia was avoiding her question about where she'd been. "I guess you guys just wanted to spend some time alone."

Claudia was silent for so long that Nancy started to think she wasn't going to answer. "Not really," she said at last. "We had a fight."

"What was it about?" Nancy asked.

After another short pause Claudia said, "He was flirting with someone. I would rather not talk about it."

Nancy decided to change the subject for the moment. "Well, everything's fine now," she said. "Listen, we want to meet Paola Rinzini. Can you arrange it?"

"Of course. She is here now," Claudia replied. "I will tell her you are coming."

When Nancy and Bess arrived at Preziosi a short while later, Claudia welcomed them, then disappeared into the back. She returned a moment later with a tall, slender woman who had jet black hair combed into a sleek pageboy.

"I'm Paola Rinzini," the woman said in good English, holding out her hand. "You wanted to speak with me?"

After Claudia introduced the two girls, Nancy turned to Paola and asked, "Could we talk in private?"

Paola lifted an eyebrow. Without a word she led the girls into her office. The back half of the large room was a storage area. The front half looked as if it was being used as an office. It held a desk, two chairs, and a bookshelf.

Paola walked behind the desk and gestured for the girls to sit. Claudia leaned against the wall while Bess and Nancy took the two chairs.

"Several pieces of Etruscan jewelry have been reported missing," Nancy began, taking a direct approach. She thought Paola's eyes narrowed a little, but she wasn't sure. "We're asking people who sell copies of Etruscan jewelry if they've seen any pieces they think might be authentic."

Paola frowned and turned to Claudia. "You know we don't sell real jewelry. Ours are inexpensive replicas." Paola gave an impatient sigh. "I'm sorry I can't help you girls."

Nancy wasn't about to give up so easily. "We purchased a necklace two days ago from Massimo

Bianco in one of the piazzas. Then we came here and tried on some of your necklaces," she explained. "Somehow, either from Massimo or this store, we walked away with a *real* Etruscan necklace."

"Massimo sold you a stolen necklace, eh?" Paola said, leaning back in her chair. "I guess we'll have to stop selling his jewelry, then. He's the only one who makes Etruscan copies for us."

"We're not sure it came from Massimo," Nancy put in quickly. "And we're not sure it's stolen—so far."

"Well, it didn't come from here," Paola said flatly, her dark eyes cold. "And I don't like what you're implying."

"Don't you even want to see the necklace?" Nancy asked.

"This is a respectable business," Paola said angrily. "We don't traffic in stolen antiquities."

Bess spoke up from the chair next to Nancy. "Would you mind if we took a look around, then? I'd like to see your jewelry up close."

Paola stood up. "Who are you?" she asked stiffly. "Are you with the police?"

"No," Nancy replied coolly. "I'd be happy to send the police if you'd prefer. Signora Fiorello asked us to find her necklace. It's been stolen."

Paola's eyes widened. "Signora Fiorello is a friend of mine. I didn't know something of hers was stolen." The store owner threw up her hands. "Fine, if you are doing this for her, look at anything you want. Just don't scare the customers."

61

Using the techniques Signor Andreotti and Massimo had shown her, Nancy examined the store's jewelry collection. Three Etruscan necklaces lay in a glass showcase, prominently displayed.

"Those are the ones from the package," Bess whispered. She looked more closely. "And that one's mine! That's the one Massimo gave me!"

"Shhh," Nancy said. "Of course the necklace he gave you would be here. After all, you did accidentally trade it for the real one."

"Do you think Paola will give it back to me?" Bess whispered. "I got so excited about the stolen necklace that I totally forgot that *I'm* out a necklace now."

"Do you think Paola Rinzini looks like the type of person who's going to give you a necklace you *say* is yours? She'd probably ask for the other necklace back."

Bess looked down at the necklace in the case longingly. "I guess you're right," she said reluctantly.

"Anyway," Nancy said, "check out the other two necklaces and see if they look real to you."

They examined each one carefully. One of the necklaces had four blue stones in it and was similar to the stolen necklace. But all three had the same clasps Massimo used, and all the beads showed traces of seams. They were definitely fakes.

The girls also searched the storeroom thoroughly but found no jewelry of any kind.

At last Nancy thanked Paola for her time and patience. "We didn't see any real jewelry," she said. "I'm sorry we bothered you."

"Well, now that you're satisfied I'm honest, you can investigate in more likely places," Paola said as she escorted Nancy and Bess to the door. "Please tell Signora Fiorello I am sorry about what happened. And that I cooperated, of course."

Claudia stepped out the door with Bess and Nancy. "I'll be right back," she told Paola.

"Whew!" Bess said once they were outside on via Condotti. "She must be loads of fun to work with."

"She is usually very pleasant," Claudia said vaguely. "I think she was offended."

"How do you know her?" Nancy asked.

She looked distractedly around, as if she was preoccupied. "Er, I know her through Signora Fiorello, actually," she finally said. "She got me the job when I told her I needed summer work."

Claudia didn't seem to be paying much attention, Nancy thought. Was it because her boss was a suspect? Or because of her fight with Sandro the night before? Or was there something else Nancy was missing?

"Listen, we wanted to stop by and see Massimo at his place," she told Claudia. "We were hoping he could show us his jewelry-making equipment." She decided it would be more prudent not to mention their real reason for going there. "Could you give us directions to his apartment?"

Claudia gave them his address in Trastevere. "It

is not far from the club where we were last night."
Then she said, "I have to go back to work. Have
fun."

Nancy and Bess rode their Vespas across the
Tiber River—*Tevere* in Italian—to Trastevere.
Buildings were crammed together along the narrow roads. Even the largest streets barely had
enough room for two cars to pass.

Massimo lived in a small, gray stone apartment
building. His name was listed outside the front
door, next to the buzzer for apartment 2A. He
didn't answer when Nancy buzzed.

"Good, he's not here," she said. She reached
into her bag for her lock-picking tools, then went
to work.

"I'll let you know if anyone's coming," Bess
offered, glancing up and down the empty street.

Nancy had the lock open a moment later, and
the girls went up the narrow stairs to the third
floor. They had learned that in Italy the ground
floor wasn't numbered. It took only another minute or so before Nancy had the door to his
apartment open, too.

Massimo's apartment had two tiny rooms and a
bathroom. Clothes, papers, and art supplies were
flung casually on every surface. Nancy and Bess
each took a room and went to work.

"He'd try to get rid of the stolen jewelry as
quickly as possible," Nancy said, thinking aloud.
"Look for something he could use to break into
the houses, or maybe a stash of money."

The girls searched for over an hour. They stumbled on a few pieces of jewelry lodged behind the bed and in the backs of drawers. Every piece proved to be a fake.

"I don't know, Nan," Bess said, brushing a strand of blond hair from her forehead. "All we've proven so far is that Massimo is a tremendous slob."

Nancy glanced over his modest furniture. "He doesn't seem to have a lot of money," she told Bess. "Certainly not as much as someone who is selling valuable antiquities."

Bess was sorting through the items scattered on Massimo's desk when she found a scrap of paper with some numbers written on it. "Look at this," she said, showing it to Nancy. "Fourteen, thirty-one, forty-three."

"Do you think that's the combination to a safe?" Nancy asked, growing excited.

"Maybe it's the combination for one that hasn't been broken into yet," Bess suggested. "Or one he's planning to rob."

Nancy found an envelope in her bag and copied the numbers onto it. "We can call Signora Fiorello and find out," she said. Staring at the figures, another idea occurred to her. "I suppose this could just be a telephone number, too. I think this is the way they write them over here."

"But I thought the numbers were seven digits."

"Some are," Nancy said. "But the older ones are only six." There was a telephone on the desk, so she picked it up and dialed the numbers.

"Pronto," a woman's voice said over the line.

Using her Italian, Nancy said, "I'm sorry, I may have the wrong number. Whose residence is this?" The woman told her, and Nancy hung up.

"Well, we've solved that mystery," Nancy told Bess, laughing. "It's Karine Azar's telephone number."

The girls burst out laughing. "He's a real operator, even if he is nice," Bess said, planting her hands on her hips. Then, more seriously, she added, "Do you think they're working together?"

"Maybe." Nancy grabbed Bess's arm and pulled her toward the door. "I can't think straight anymore. Let's take a break, okay? Why don't we grab a pizza and see a movie?"

Bess grinned. "As long as it has English subtitles, or you translate, you're on."

For the first time since arriving in Rome, Nancy and Bess wandered through Trastevere as true tourists. After watching a horror movie, they stopped in a piazza ringed with restaurants. Chairs and tables spilled out from each restaurant, filling the piazza. The girls ordered a thin, garlic-covered pizza with a smear of tomato sauce and stayed until the evening lights came on. They got back to their pensione just after dark.

As Nancy and Bess were walking past the front desk, Signora Verona stuck her head out from behind the curtain. "A Signora Fiorello called for you about ten minutes ago," she told the girls. "She wants you right away."

Nancy called from the lobby phone. The phone only rang once before Sandro's mother answered.

"Nancy! Thank goodness you called," Signora Fiorello exclaimed. "Something terrible happened."

"Are you all right?" Nancy asked. "Did something happen to Sandro?"

"No, no, we are fine. But another piece of Etruscan jewelry has been stolen!"

Chapter

Seven

"OH, NO!" NANCY CRIED.

Quickly, she found out what had happened. The theft had occurred at a friend's house, according to Sandro's mother. Signora De Luca had come home after a party to find her Etruscan pin missing. She had called the police and then Signora Fiorello, who had told her about Nancy.

Nancy got the woman's address and promised to go over to the house right away.

"Sandro's there, so he can introduce you," Signora Fiorello told her. "He was visiting my friend's son Carlo when she discovered what had happened."

Did Sandro just happen to be around? Nancy wondered as she hung up.

After she told Bess what had happened, the girls hurried to the De Luca residence on their Vespas.

Sandro and a swarthy young man who introduced himself as Carlo answered the door.

Nancy saw that the police were still there. She recognized Officer Franchi, who was talking to an elegant woman in a red silk suit. Nancy guessed that she must be Signora De Luca.

Going over to the couch where the woman was sitting, Sandro introduced Nancy and Bess. Officer Franchi's mouth twisted with resentment, but Signora De Luca insisted they stay. Thwarted, the police officer escorted them around the crime scene.

Speaking in Italian, he showed Nancy the safe behind one of the armchairs in the parlor, telling her an Etruscan pin had been stolen from it that afternoon. He went on to explain that Signora De Luca opened her safe earlier to get a pair of earrings to wear. Sandro and her son Carlo were at the house until five. When they came back three hours later, Signora De Luca was just returning. She went straight to her safe to return her earrings and discovered that the pin was gone.

The confusion on Bess's face made it clear that she wasn't picking up much of the story, but Nancy didn't have time to explain right then. She leaned forward to study the safe. There were no scratches or fingerprints. The alarm system hadn't been set off or tampered with. Nothing seemed to have been disturbed.

"We have a number of reports of missing jewelry," Officer Franchi said, still speaking in Italian. He fixed Nancy with a piercing look. "I don't suppose you know anything about that."

"I've heard about them," Nancy told him. "But I haven't found out anything concrete. Fabio Andreotti offered to buy all the stolen jewelry, though. What do you know about him?"

"He has an excellent reputation," Officer Franchi told her. "We've never had any problems with him."

Nancy nodded. "So you think it's just a coincidence that his name keeps popping up?"

"Artifacts and jewelry are his business. But if you find anything more, let me know." Officer Franchi's dark eyes swept over Nancy. "I called the River Heights police department. You're very respected in your country. I'm sure you'll let me know if you uncover any leads."

It was after ten o'clock by the time the police left, but Signora De Luca asked Nancy and Bess to stay behind. Over iced tea and *biscòtti* the De Lucas and Sandro repeated their accounts of the evening for the girls.

"Who knew you were going out?" Nancy asked Signora De Luca when they were done.

"The people at the reception," the woman replied, speaking in heavily accented English. "But all of my friends know Carlo is here. No one could know the house was empty."

"How about the doorman? Do you trust him?" Bess asked. She looked grateful to be hearing English again.

Signora De Luca nodded forcefully. "He has worked here for years. The police spoke to him."

Turning to Sandro and Carlo, Nancy said, "You were here for two hours after Signora De Luca left.

Could anyone have gotten in without your noticing?"

"No one was here when we were," said Carlo.

"Well, did anyone know you wouldn't be here?" Nancy asked.

Sandro took a bite of a *biscòtto* and explained, "We were going to watch television with Massimo, but we got hungry and decided to go out instead. No one could have predicted that."

So once again Massimo was connected in some way. "Where is Massimo now?" Nancy asked.

"He didn't come with us," Carlo said. "When I told him we wanted to go out, he changed his mind."

There was nothing suspicious about that, Nancy thought, unless you added it to all the other little clues pointing to Massimo. She and Bess hadn't found any jewelry in his apartment, but Nancy supposed he could be keeping it somewhere else.

Nancy's eyes narrowed as she looked at Sandro. Was all of his concern about the jewelry just an act? she wondered. After all, being in the apartment as a guest gave him pretty good access to the safe.

Nancy shook herself. It looked as if one person was responsible for all the thefts, and she seriously doubted that Sandro would steal a necklace from his own mother.

She and Bess chatted with the De Lucas and Sandro while they finished their iced tea, but no one could shed any more light on the evening's events. After promising to call Signora De Luca the minute they uncovered anything, the girls left.

As she rode back to their pensione Nancy felt frustrated. She hadn't unearthed a single clue in this case. There were never any signs of forced entry and no telltale marks on the safes. It was as if a ghost were pulling off the thefts.

Nancy was exhausted, but that night she couldn't get to sleep. She tossed in bed, trying to figure out how everyone fit into the latest crime. Massimo knew the apartment would be empty. Was it more than a coincidence that he had canceled his plans to join Sandro and Carlo? And where did Sandro and Claudia fit in? They had been acting weird, too.

Nancy groaned, throwing her arm over her face as she rolled over in the twisted sheets yet again. How was she ever going to get to the bottom of this case?

"Boy, I don't know how I'm going to be able to leave Rome and give up eating those delicious pastries every morning," Bess said the following morning as she and Nancy finished their breakfast at the café near their pensione. "So what do we do today?"

Nancy stifled a yawn. Even though she had slept late, she didn't feel very rested. This case was starting to get to her. "We could try to find out where the stolen jewelry is going," she suggested. "I also want to go back to Preziosi to look into the store's finances. They don't seem to have many customers, did you notice?"

After breakfast Nancy called Claudia at the

store. "Are you busy right now?" Nancy asked. "I wanted to ask you a couple of questions."

"Not that busy," Claudia told her. "Things are quiet, and Paola is out looking at merchandise this morning."

"Actually, I was going to ask how well the store is doing," Nancy said. "But if Paola's not there . . ."

"You want to see the accounting books?" Claudia guessed. She hesitated, then said, "If you come now, it will be okay. Paola won't be back until after lunch."

"We're on our way," Nancy said, then hung up.

Claudia was helping a customer when Nancy and Bess arrived. She motioned for them to go into the back, then returned to the woman who was looking at leather bags.

In the back room Nancy saw a ledger sitting in the center of Paola's desk. Claudia had obviously pulled it out for them.

"That was my first sale of the day," Claudia said a moment later, joining Nancy and Bess. "Lately sales are even slower than usual."

She sat down at Paola's desk and gestured to the ledger. "Before you came I looked through this book to see if I could see anything that did not look right, but it is pretty much the usual business stuff. No large sums of money."

"So if she's selling stolen jewelry over the counter, the books don't show it," Bess said. "Not that you would expect them to."

Nancy had been glancing at the figures, trying to

make sense of them. "If I'm reading this thing correctly, these numbers don't show a bustling business either," she observed. "The store is barely breaking even."

"The rents on via Condotti are very high," Claudia said with a sigh. "The tourist trade is not enough to carry us anymore. Paola is trying to change our merchandise to attract more local customers."

"So she may need more money to keep the store afloat," Nancy said. "But so far we can't prove any of the stolen jewelry has been here. Oh—by the way, you haven't seen any Etruscan pins come in today, have you?" she asked.

Seeing Claudia's blank look, Nancy told her about Signora De Luca's pin. As she talked Claudia grew visibly more distressed.

"So the thief is still at work," she said. "Sandro did not tell me a thing about this latest theft. We must do something!"

Nancy was also surprised that Sandro hadn't mentioned anything to Claudia. "Did you talk to him last night?" she asked.

"No," Claudia said, a little too quickly.

Nancy looked at Claudia closely for a moment, then said, "Well, we need to know more about where the stolen jewelry is going. Who's buying it? And is it being sold in Italy or smuggled out?"

Bess seemed perplexed. "You mean learning that might help us figure out who the thief is?" she asked. "But that seems like pretty specialized information. How can we find it out?"

"You need to talk to an expert," Claudia said.

"What about Fabio Andreotti? I know you suspect him, but I cannot imagine him stealing."

Nancy was doubtful, but she decided to go along with Claudia's suggestion. If nothing else, it would give her a chance to find out more about how Andreotti himself might be involved in the thefts.

The girls set out on their Vespas to catch Signor Andreotti at his office. Claudia piggybacked behind Nancy, giving her directions through the back streets, while Bess rode behind them. They were still several blocks away when Nancy felt Claudia's grip tighten.

"There he is!" she exclaimed in Nancy's ear.

Nancy stopped, waving for Bess to pull up alongside. "There *who* is?" she asked Claudia.

"Fabio Andreotti," Claudia replied. She gave a meaningful nod across the street. "At the café."

Nancy spotted Fabio Andreotti seated at an outdoor table under an umbrella. He was engaged in a lively conversation with a woman seated across from him, his smile lighting up his stern, chiseled features. The woman's back was to the girls.

"Who's he talking to?" Bess wondered aloud.

"Maybe we should go closer to get a better look," Claudia suggested.

The three girls rode slowly down the road until they could see the woman's profile. Claudia did a double-take when she saw the woman.

"What is Paola doing here? She is supposed to be looking at merchandise," she said in confusion. "I had no idea they knew each other."

This was news to Nancy, too. As the girls

watched, Paola picked up a small fabric Preziosi sack near her chair and drew a package partially out of it, showing it to Andreotti. Then she slipped the package back and handed him the whole bag.

Fabio Andreotti looked around him, an uncomfortable expression on his face. He started to say something, but Paola put her finger to her lips to silence him. Then, as the girls watched, she put on a pair of sunglasses, stood, and disappeared into the street!

Chapter
Eight

Do you think that—" Bess began.

"That was a rendezvous to pass off stolen goods?" Nancy finished the question for her.

The three girls looked at one another. "Maybe it is the pin you were talking about," Claudia suggested.

Bess grabbed Nancy's arm. "We have to get it before he can dispose of it!" she cried.

"He's paying the check now," Nancy said as the art dealer rose. "Let's follow him."

Signor Andreotti strolled down the street, swinging the sack Paola had given him. The girls drove their Vespas slowly on the opposite side, keeping behind him. A few blocks later they realized he was going back to his office.

"Let's get there first and just 'happen' to run into him in the lobby," Nancy suggested. "Then he won't have time to get rid of that bag."

Speeding past Signor Andreotti, they parked their Vespas near his office. They made a dash for the lobby. A few minutes later the art dealer sauntered into the building.

"Claudia! And your charming friends," he greeted them easily in his good English. "Have you brought your necklace to sell?"

"We're actually here for some advice," Nancy said, making up her story as she went along. "We wanted to talk to you over lunch."

Signor Andreotti smiled. "It would have been a pleasure, but I've eaten. Why don't you come up to my office instead?"

The girls exchanged silent glances as they got into the elevator with him. Once they were all seated in his office, the art dealer said, "Four pretty young women in one day is a treat for me." He put the sack he was carrying into a desk drawer.

"Who is the fourth?" Claudia asked coyly. "There are only three of us here."

"Paola Rinzini," the art dealer replied. "Do you know her?"

Well, Nancy thought with surprise, he wasn't trying to hide his association with Paola. "Claudia works at Paola's store," she put in.

"You two are friends?" Claudia asked.

Signor Andreotti smiled. "Just friends," he said. "She comes to me for advice, too."

"She has Etruscan necklaces to sell?" Nancy asked, trying to keep her tone light.

Signor Andreotti gave Nancy a look of mild surprise and shook his head. "No, but she is very interested in them. She wants to open a gallery, so I'm teaching her about antiquities."

"Really," Claudia said, leaning forward. "But she would be your competition then, wouldn't she?"

Signor Andreotti gave a confident wave of his hand. "I have lifelong customers," he said. "I don't have to worry about Paola Rinzini at all."

Nancy's mind was going in another direction. If Preziosi was barely breaking even, she thought, Paola would have to have another source of income to open her gallery—such as selling stolen Etruscan jewelry, for example.

Of course, there was still the possibility that Andreotti was lying and was really helping Paola traffic her stolen goods. She still hadn't seen what was in the sack Paola had given him.

"I noticed you came in with a Preziosi bag," Nancy said casually. "Claudia, do you think it could be the pin?"

Claudia looked at Nancy in alarm, obviously not knowing how to respond.

Turning back to Signor Andreotti, Nancy quickly improvised. "This morning a customer's package was switched by accident. She bought a fake Etruscan pin, but when she got home she had a scarf instead," she said smoothly. "Claudia turned the store upside down looking for that pin. Finally we figured it must have been put into another bag by mistake."

She gave the dealer a shy smile. "Perhaps Paola gave you that bag. She could have taken the pin by accident."

"I haven't even looked in it," Signor Andreotti said. "It's a gift, for my advice on her gallery. I told her it wasn't necessary."

"Well, would you mind checking for us? Just to be sure?" Bess asked, picking up on Nancy's ruse.

Signor Andreotti pulled the fabric sack out of his drawer. Taking a small, flat package from it, he carefully split the tape holding the lid closed, then pulled it off.

Nestled inside the box was a beautiful leather belt.

Claudia gave a deep sigh, making Nancy realize she had also been holding her breath. It looked as if Signor Andreotti was telling the truth.

"I guess someone else has the pin," Claudia said slowly. She looked even more dejected than Nancy felt.

"I hope you find it," Signor Andreotti said, putting the belt back in the drawer. "Now, how can I help you girls?"

The vague moodiness Nancy had detected in Claudia earlier seemed to have returned. Claudia got up abruptly. "I think Nancy has something to ask," she said, moving toward the door. "Unfortunately, I have to get back to the store."

Claudia barely waved goodbye, and then she was out the door. She hadn't been her usual cheerful self that day, Nancy thought. And seeing the belt had made her even more glum than before. It was almost as if she was disappointed that Fabio Andreotti wasn't the thief. Nancy couldn't shake the feeling that Claudia was hiding something, but she had no idea what. Or maybe she was just ashamed that her detective friends couldn't seem to crack this case.

Signor Andreotti was looking at her expectantly, Nancy realized. She took a deep breath, then said, "I'm not sure if you're aware of this, but someone is stealing Etruscan jewelry out of people's homes."

She and Bess told him about everything, including the fact that someone had ransacked their room. "Since you're a dealer," Nancy concluded, "we thought you might be able to help us. We were hoping to uncover a clue as to where the jewelry could be going."

The art dealer's initial expression of surprise had changed to one of close interest while Nancy talked. "Well!" he said now. "So this is the mystery behind your necklace." Nancy and Bess nodded.

"The jewelry is almost certainly being smuggled out of the country," Andreotti continued. "Each piece is one of a kind. They would be easy to spot, even in Milan or Florence."

"How could they be smuggled out of the country?" Nancy asked.

The art dealer considered her question for a moment. "One way is to send it out with regular shipments sent by a legal company. Then the jewelry would be very difficult to detect."

"What kind of company?" Bess asked.

"Any company that ships out of the country. One that exports wine, for example."

That didn't exactly narrow down the number of possible choices, Nancy realized. The three of them fell into a thoughtful silence. Signor Andreotti finally spoke up.

"Why don't you set a trap?" he suggested, his eyes twinkling. "Tempt the thief with something he or she can't refuse."

Nancy frowned. "But if we don't know who the thief is, how can we lure the person into a trap?"

"Let me think," said the art dealer, tapping his fingertips on his desk. "There's a gala tomorrow night for a very talented artist who is having a big show. Perhaps we could set something up."

Bess jumped on the idea. "You mean, arrange for someone to wear an Etruscan necklace?"

"Yes, and I know just the right person!" Signor Andreotti said triumphantly. "A friend of mine is visiting from France. I even have the perfect necklace for her to wear. I am sure she would be happy to be a—how do you call it?—decoy."

Signor Andreotti and the girls excitedly pieced together their trap. In the middle of the planning Nancy sat back in her chair and slapped her forehead.

"Wait a minute. How can we be sure that the thief will be among the guests?"

"It's the right crowd," Signor Andreotti said, showing her the list. Nancy didn't know most of the names, but several of the women who had been burglarized were listed, including Sandro's mother. Paola Rinzini's name was penciled in at the bottom.

"I invited Paola at lunch," Signor Andreotti explained. "Give me a list of people you suspect, and I will add them. I'm one of the hosts, so I'm sure there won't be a problem."

Nancy wrote down her name and Bess's. Then she added Claudia, Sandro, Massimo, and after a moment, Karine Azar. When Signor Andreotti saw the list, he whistled.

"It's a good thing our artist is very young. I can say I invited you to generate excitement about the show among the younger generation."

After they had gone over all the details of the plan Signor Andreotti recommended a few stores for the girls to visit to buy items they would need the following night.

As the girls got up to leave he said, "I'm glad you came to me. I would do anything I could to help my friends and to keep our treasured antiquities here in Italy. Besides," he added, ushering them to the door, "this is the most fun I've had in years!"

When Nancy and Bess returned to Pensione Antonio, Bess paused at the telephone. "Maybe we should call Claudia," she said to Nancy. "I mean, she's been so nice to us. I hate to think of her as a suspect now. Maybe there's a simple explanation for how she acted today."

"Good idea," Nancy agreed. She found one last *gettóne* in her purse, plunked it into the pay phone, and dialed Claudia's home number.

When Claudia answered, Nancy greeted her, then said, "Claudia, you seemed upset in Signor Andreotti's office. Is anything wrong?"

There was a short silence. "I guess I was hoping

this thing would be over." Claudia's voice finally came over the line. "I feel responsible for dragging you into this. I took you to Massimo's stand and the store, and all of a sudden people are losing their jewelry!"

"But most of the jewelry was probably stolen before we even got to Rome," Nancy said. "Listen, Signor Andreotti was a big help. He even invited us all to some gala tomorrow night for a young artist. He said he thought it would be fun, and he's putting Sandro, Massimo, Karine, and you on the list, too. Won't that be great?"

Nancy didn't give away the real reason they were all being invited. She couldn't if there was any chance that Claudia was somehow involved in the thefts.

"Great," Claudia said, but her tone was flat.

Taking a deep breath, Nancy decided to make one last effort. "Claudia, you sound terrible. Please tell me what's wrong."

"It is just this silly fight with Sandro," Claudia said, her voice breaking slightly. "It is nothing to worry about. By the way, Massimo and Sandro and I want to take you and Bess sightseeing tomorrow. There is a special church we think you will enjoy."

The girls arranged to meet at the Spanish Steps the next morning. After hanging up, Nancy and Bess dropped off their purchases in their room, then changed into dresses for dinner. They decided to splurge on one of the better restaurants listed in their guidebook.

* * *

"Boy, I think that was the best veal I ever tasted," Bess said afterward as they wandered through the streets near the Pantheon, where the restaurant was located.

The streets and piazzas were packed with young people hanging out. As they walked Nancy pulled out her guidebook and flipped to the "Eating Out" section.

"Are you up for dessert?" she asked Bess. "There's an ice-cream place near here that's supposed to be great. It's called Giolitti."

Bess's blue eyes lit up. "Say no more—let's go!"

It was obvious that Giolitti was very popular. When the girls arrived, it was packed with locals and tourists alike. Dozens of colorful flavors were set out in stainless steel drums. Men in waiters' jackets pushed one another out of the way, scooping the *gelato* neatly with spatulas.

Bess read the flavors. *"Gianduia, crèma, pistàcchio, cioccolato,"* she said, throwing her hands in the air. "I can't figure this out! I'm just going to pick a color." A cone piled high with ice cream and fresh whipped cream passed near her nose. "And I'm getting the cream."

The *gelato* was the most delicious ice cream Nancy had ever tasted. Fully satisfied, the girls headed back to their pensione.

"I'm beat," Nancy said as she unlocked the door to their room and pushed it open.

As she stepped into their room she was startled by the sight of a dark shape on her bed. "Don't come in, Bess," she ordered, freezing in place.

When the shape didn't move, she reached out slowly and turned on the light.

Bess gave a little screech.

In the middle of Nancy's bed sat a gruesome stone gargoyle's head. Next to it was a slip of paper with words scrawled on it in red paint.

Nancy's stomach lurched as she read the jagged writing: "Rome is a crumbling city. Get away before it crumbles on you!"

Chapter

Nine

"OH, NAN, THE THIEF is really after us," Bess whispered, her face white.

"Well, he's going to be disappointed, then," Nancy said grimly. "I don't scare easily."

Gingerly she reached out and touched the head. It rocked slightly on the mattress but was surprisingly light. Nancy lifted it easily and carried it closer to the light. The head seemed to be made of some sort of dense foam. Nancy lifted it easily and carried it closer to the light. The head seemed to be made of some sort of dense foam.

"More threats," Bess said gloomily. "That at least means we're getting closer, right? I guess I should be happy."

"But who is the thief we spooked?" Nancy wondered. "Both Fabio Andreotti and Paola Rinzini know we're on the trail now. And Massimo, Sandro, and Claudia all know we've been investigating."

Coming over to Nancy, Bess made a face at the gargoyle. "Where does a person find a head like that in Rome?" she asked.

"It could be a stage prop of some kind, or a model," Nancy said. She set the head down on the dresser. "Or maybe it could have come from an art school."

The two girls looked at each other. "Massimo and Karine both go to art school," Bess put in.

"Well, let's see if we can track down the culprit this time," Nancy said. The two girls went down the hall and found Signora Verona sitting behind the desk. When Nancy finished telling her what had happened, the pensione manager was beside herself.

"Someone in my family has been watching that door all day," she told the girls. "We even made a new rule: guests may not have visitors in the rooms." She gestured to a hand-drawn sign above the front desk. "No one has been in or out of here unless they have a room."

"The head is pretty large," Nancy observed. "It would be hard to smuggle in, except in a big bag. Did anyone check into the hotel today?"

The woman looked through her records. "A German family checked into room seven this morning," she told them. "And a young man from Milan arrived this afternoon."

Nancy jumped on the information. "Was he Italian? Can you remember what he looked like?"

Signora Verona narrowed her eyes in concentration. "He was attractive. I think I remember black hair, kind of wavy, but he was wearing a hat. I thought that was strange for the summer. He had one duffel bag."

Massimo had wavy black hair! Nancy thought with excitement. "Which room is he in?" Nancy asked. "I'd like to ask him about this."

"Room three, at the end of the hall. He gave the name Francesco Ponti."

While the girls followed Signora Verona down the hall Nancy translated for Bess everything the pensione manager had told her. "Massimo again," Bess said under her breath. "It's looking more and more like he's our thief."

Nancy and Bess waited silently while Signora Verona knocked on the door to room three. There was no answer.

"Could you open the door with a passkey?" Nancy asked. "Please? This is important."

The woman hesitated only for a moment. She went to the front desk and came back with the key. Nancy held her breath as the door opened.

The room was untouched. There were no belongings in sight. A skeleton key on a wooden tag lay on the neatly made bed. "Francesco Ponti" was gone!

The next morning Nancy and Bess got up very early. They took the threatening note and the key down to the police station and left them for Officer Franchi, telling the officer on duty what had happened. Then they hurried back to the Spanish Steps to meet the others.

Claudia and Sandro were already sitting on a lower step when Nancy and Bess arrived, just before nine. They weren't speaking, and Claudia still looked upset.

Bess had noticed it, too. She kept up a stream of chatter just to ease the tension a little. Suddenly Bess broke off, and her mouth fell open. Following Bess's gaze, Nancy saw that Massimo was approaching the group—with Karine!

"Hi, everyone," Karine said in her musical voice. "When Massimo told me last night where you were going, I made him promise to bring me." She flashed a brilliant smile. "I hope no one minds."

Nancy noticed that Karine emphasized the words "last night" as if she wanted everyone to know that she and Massimo had been out together.

"We're delighted to have you," Bess said, noticing Massimo's awkward posture.

"And I hope you're coming to that art opening tonight, too," Nancy put in. "Were you invited?"

Karine looked down at her nails as she answered. "I received a note from Signor Andreotti that some young people were going and I should come along," she said. "But I was going with my father, anyway. He was invited weeks ago."

Massimo and Sandro spoke up; both were obviously happy about being invited to the opening. Nancy got the impression that they didn't usually attend this sort of fancy affair.

With an uneasy look at Karine, Massimo turned to Bess and took her by the arm. "Now let me tell you what we are going to see today," he told her.

As Nancy watched them walk ahead, she hoped Bess would ask him where he had been yesterday afternoon at around the time Signora De Luca's Etruscan pin was stolen. Claudia didn't seem to be interested in being with Sandro, so Nancy paired up with her. Sandro and Karine lagged behind.

Keeping her voice low, Nancy told Claudia about the gargoyle head, leaving out the part about the mysterious Francesco Ponti.

"But that is terrible!" Claudia exclaimed. "Were you hurt? Was anything stolen?"

"I still have the necklace," Nancy said, patting her purse. "It may have been a prank."

As the group wandered down via Sistina, Claudia walked silently next to Nancy, darting glances at Sandro every few steps. Finally Nancy touched her arm. "Why don't you go talk to him?"

Claudia gave a wan smile. "Maybe I should." Nancy fell into step with Karine so that Claudia and Sandro could be alone. Trying to strike up a conversation, Nancy asked Karine to tell her about the sights they passed as they walked.

"This is the Triton Fountain," Karine said as the group stopped in the Piazza Barberini. Perched atop an open shell supported by four dolphins, a stone figure on his knees spouted water through a large seashell. The water dribbled a lazy path through the mossy rivulets on his chest.

"Do you draw statues like this one?" Nancy asked Karine as they walked on.

"Sometimes, but the gray chalk doesn't always come out so well on the pavement. I like color."

91

"I'd like to see your drawings. Maybe sometime you'd draw that famous Botticelli painting of Venus standing in the shell. What's it called?"

Karine made a knowing nod. *"The Birth of Venus,"* she replied. "But I never take requests. I just draw whatever moves me at the moment.

"Actually," Karine continued after Nancy didn't respond, "I draw for my father when he asks me to."

"It's nice that he visits you in the piazza to see your work," Nancy commented. "Not all parents are so involved in their kids' careers."

"He isn't," Karine said. "He's too busy for that. My father owns a big trading company. But sometimes he calls me in the morning to see what I'm up to. He likes to visualize what I'm doing during the day."

Nancy looked at Karine, puzzled. "Your father calls you on the telephone in the morning?" she asked.

"My parents are divorced," Karine explained. "I live with my mother. My father's got his own import-export company in Turkey and a small apartment here in Rome. He travels back and forth a lot, so I see him only when he's here."

"I'm sorry," Nancy said, not knowing what else to say.

Karine shrugged and changed the subject. "Did Bess find her necklace—the one Massimo gave her?"

"We haven't worked that out yet," Nancy said vaguely, wondering why Karine was so interested.

"I'd love to see it when you do. Massimo's going

to give me a necklace, too," Karine added smugly. "With green stones to match my eyes."

Nancy tried not to laugh. "A necklace to match your eyes" seemed to be a standard pickup line for Massimo.

By now the group found itself on the corner of via Veneto. They stopped in front of a small stone church.

"Inside are the catacombs of the Capuchin monks," Massimo said. "They are not Rome's most famous tourist attraction, but I think they are the most unusual."

He led the group up a flight of stairs along the right of the church to the first landing aboveground. Two short monks dressed in brown and white robes were selling postcards in a small reception area.

A long hallway beyond the monks led to a bizarre burial ground. It was arranged in five small chapels, connected by a long passage. The walls were entirely covered with bones!

"Ugh!" Bess said. "This is really creepy."

"This is a holy burial ground for four thousand monks," Massimo explained.

To Nancy it was a grisly sight. Every wall was decorated with the bones of the monks. She gave a little shiver as she looked around. Leg bones were fastened in a pattern on the ceiling. Skulls alternated with arm bones down the walls. Even the lamp holders were made of bones. In the nearest chapel Nancy could see three full skeletons dressed in monks' robes, holding crosses.

"It was an honor to be buried here," Massimo

said in a low voice. "The living monks decorated each chapel with the bones of their brothers. They think the custom was introduced by the Etruscans."

Nancy looked sharply at Massimo. He was smiling at Bess, forgetting Nancy for the moment.

Despite the summer heat, the rooms were cool. Sandro wandered down the hall, examining each part of the wall in horrified fascination. Other members of the group drifted after him. They seemed to be the only visitors.

Nancy wandered into an empty chapel in the middle of the hall and stared. A monk's skeleton was propped up in the middle of a design made of human foot bones. Stepping closer, Nancy tried to glimpse the skull under the brown monk's hood.

There were quiet footsteps behind Nancy as someone entered the chapel. "Isn't it fascinating?" she asked, still gazing at the skeleton.

No one answered. Suddenly Nancy tensed. Before she could turn, she felt an arm cover her eyes and a hand cover her mouth.

Nancy struggled, trying to get free. In the next instant she felt herself being pulled off balance, then pushed with great force. As she fell forward she felt a tug where her bag hung from her shoulder.

She didn't have time to fight or even see who her attacker was, however. She was hurtling right into the wall of bones. In a split second she was going to crash into the skeleton of the monk!

Chapter
Ten

NANCY PITCHED HEADLONG into the skeleton, bringing it down around her as she fell. Brown bones scattered everywhere, producing a light cloud of dust.

In panic Nancy struggled to get away from the bones, yelling for help. She was dimly aware of the sound of a door slamming behind her.

Dizzy from her fall, Nancy scrambled toward the doorway, taking a mental inventory of her body as she went. She had smashed her elbow against the wall, but otherwise she felt all right. A heavy wooden door barred the exit from the chapel, though. The thief had slammed the door shut behind him, and now she found that it was stuck. She began shouting and pounding on the door.

"Nancy, are you in there?" Claudia shouted through the door a few minutes later.

95

"Yes, I'm here," she called back.

She was relieved when the door opened a moment later and the group piled into the room. Claudia was holding a piece of splintered wood.

"This was jammed against the door," she said, her horrified gaze sweeping the tumble of bones around her. "What happened?"

Nancy described the attack as best she could. Everyone exclaimed over her, but no one had seen anything. From what they told her, they had each been off looking at a different part of the catacombs. None of them had an alibi.

"I have never heard of a tourist being mugged in a church before," Claudia said indignantly. "I am ashamed for our whole city."

"I think it was a deliberate attempt to get the necklace," Nancy said. "Unfortunately, it worked."

Bess gasped. "Your shoulder bag is gone!" she exclaimed, but Nancy's eyes darted to the others, trying to gauge their reactions. Claudia, Massimo, and Sandro all looked horrified. Karine was the only one who didn't seem upset by the news.

"This is too dangerous," Sandro said. "I know you're trying to help my mother, but she wouldn't want you to get hurt. I think you should leave this to the police."

Nancy started toward the door. "I'll definitely report this attack," she agreed. "But I'm not backing off the case."

She went to the monks at the entrance, who conducted her to a back office to use the phone. Officer Franchi was out, so she told the officer on duty what had happened and described her bag and its contents. Then she sat in the office collecting her thoughts.

Now that the thief had made such an obvious and dangerous move, Nancy felt as if she must be closing in. She was sure that the person who had just attacked her was a man, which meant that he was either Massimo or Sandro. And Massimo fit the description of the mysterious Francesco Ponti better than Sandro. The question now was, what would the thief do with her bag and the necklace?

When Nancy came out of the office, the others were searching for her shoulder bag. She eyed the various bags her friends were carrying. Should she search them?

She decided against it. Doing so would certainly offend them and might scare off the thief before the gala that evening. But she'd be on the lookout for a way to search them during the day.

"We didn't find your purse anywhere," Claudia told Nancy apologetically as the group prepared to leave the catacombs.

Nancy let out a sigh. "I'm more upset about the necklace than about any of my stuff," she said. "Still, it's not going to be fun getting a new passport and credit cards."

Coming over to Nancy, Massimo put an arm around her shoulders. "Well, I know something that *would* be fun," he told her. "I was thinking we could go to the soccer match between Rome and Turin."

"Soccer!" Bess crowed. "I love soccer!"

Nancy shot Bess an amused look. The only

sports Bess had ever liked were shopping and dating. She obviously wanted to spend more time with Massimo, even if she wasn't interested in a romance.

"That's a great idea," Nancy said quickly. "I can deal with replacing my cards tomorrow." And, she added silently, now she could keep her eye on Massimo and the others to see if they made a move with the necklace.

"Soccer in Italy is a real event," Claudia chimed in. "But what about lunch?"

The teens grabbed some *panini* and headed for the Foro Italico, where the soccer match was taking place. Flags and banners in bright colors waved everywhere. Turin's fans were decked out in black and white, while the Romans wore yellow and red.

As the group made its way to the seats the crowd surged with each kick and play. Chants of "Juve!" and "Roma!" were traded back and forth.

"What's *'Juve'?*" Bess shouted above the din.

"It stands for Juventus," Sandro explained. "That's the name of the Turin team. And Rom—"

"Is the Roman team," Bess finished for him. "I get it. These people are serious sports fans."

"Sometimes too serious," Claudia said, nodding. She was sitting next to Sandro, holding his arm, Nancy noticed. She didn't seem angry with him anymore. "Terrible things can happen at soccer games when the fans get out of hand."

"Great. Does that mean we're going to be attacked if we shout the wrong thing?" Bess asked.

"I think Nancy's been attacked enough for one day!"

The crowd was on its feet, screaming for a goal. Sandro explained the game to Bess while Massimo, who was standing between Nancy and Karine, pointed out the favorite Roman players.

When Turin got the ball Massimo quietly excused himself. Nancy watched him disappear.

Could he be meeting someone? she wondered. She climbed over the people in her row and followed him. Maybe he was getting rid of the necklace!

Massimo was standing near one of the refreshment stands, sipping a soda. Nancy waited for something to happen, but to her surprise Massimo finished the drink, then bought a few more and headed back to the group.

Had he just waited until he finished so that he could carry more sodas back? Or had he been waiting for someone who never showed up? He didn't have his backpack with him, she noticed. Maybe he didn't have the necklace on him after all, she thought. His polo shirt had no pockets, and Nancy doubted he could be concealing the necklace in his tight jeans.

Once back in his seat Massimo became a boisterous fan, yelling "Roma" joyfully with the crowd. At halftime he excused himself to use the restroom and again left his backpack behind.

This time Nancy wanted to search the backpack. "Does Massimo have some sunglasses?" she asked Karine, who was sitting on the other side of

Massimo's empty seat. "The glare is hurting my eyes." Without waiting for an answer Nancy unzipped the backpack and thrust her hand in. "He won't mind if I borrow them," she said sweetly.

While she pretended to rummage for the glasses Nancy searched the backpack thoroughly. Bess's necklace wasn't there, nor did she see any other Etruscan jewelry.

"No glasses," she said, replacing the backpack and smiling at Karine. "Oh, well."

Could Massimo have hidden the necklace in the catacombs, expecting to get it later? It would be fairly safe hidden among the bones. Or maybe Sandro had it. He and Claudia seemed to have made up. Did that have anything to do with the necklace?

A sudden roar went up from the crowd behind her. Nancy looked at the field, wondering if the teams were coming back on for the second half. Nothing was happening on the field, but the commotion behind Nancy was growing. Massimo's voice rang out loudly.

Turning, Nancy saw him barreling through the stands about ten rows behind them. An angry pack of Turin fans wearing black and white were on his heels.

Nancy yelled out a warning as Massimo dodged seats and fans, pushing people out of the way. He was headed straight for them—and going too fast to stop!

Chapter

Eleven

SANDRO LEAPT OVER NANCY and grabbed Massimo, breaking his fall. The group chasing Massimo launched themselves into the seated Roman fans, and a brawl began.

Bess screamed and scrambled after Claudia to one side, away from the flying fists. Nancy and Karine grabbed their things in a rush and followed them.

Several police officers appeared out of nowhere, swarming over the spectators to separate them. They pulled Massimo and three Turin fans apart as everyone shouted his own version of what had happened. Italian phrases flew too quickly for Nancy to keep up. The police released Massimo and Sandro but kept the Turin fans firmly between them.

Finally Massimo and Sandro came back to the group. Massimo put his hand to his mouth, nursing a split lip, but otherwise he was fine. Both he and Sandro were glowing with victory.

"They were screaming insults when I walked by," Massimo explained as they all sat back down again, "so I said a few things about their team. I guess they could make insults but not take them."

"We should put some ice on that," Karine said, touching Massimo's lip.

"The game is starting again," he objected. "I want to see us win!"

Claudia leaned over Sandro to talk to Bess and Nancy. "I told you it gets serious sometimes," she said as the soccer teams spilled back out onto the field. "These fans are so competitive!"

Nancy enjoyed the rest of the game. Rome won, three to one. When it was over the group dispersed, planning to meet at the art gala that evening. As Massimo and Karine walked off Nancy saw Karine slip her arm around Massimo's waist and give him a hug.

Bess was watching, too. "When we were walking to the catacombs, I told him not to worry about dating Karine," she said. "After all, I *am* going off to Greece, then back home."

When Nancy and Bess got back to the hotel, there was a message from Officer Franchi informing Nancy that her shoulder bag had been found in a trash can right near the catacombs. Her wallet, money, and passport were all still there, but the necklace was missing.

"I guess it's official," Nancy said ruefully after she hung up. "It was our necklace thief, all right. A regular thief would have taken my money."

Bess bit her lip as she and Nancy went to their room. "Maybe if he's got your necklace, he won't want another one," she said thoughtfully. "What if he doesn't take the bait tonight?"

"He will," Nancy said confidently. "Signor Andreotti said he'll use his most expensive necklace. Our thief won't be able to resist."

"I can't believe we didn't ruin our dresses," Bess said, smoothing the skirt of her purple silk minidress after she and Nancy had parked their Vespas outside the entrance to the building where the gala was being held. The spaghetti straps exposed Bess's shoulders and showed off her tan.

"I can't believe we made it on time, considering all I had to do," Nancy added.

Before leaving for the gala Nancy had claimed her purse at the police station and then taken the clothes she and Bess would need later that night to the Belvedere Hotel. She had really had to rush in order to get dressed on time, but she was pleased with the result. Her pale aqua dress set off her reddish blond hair perfectly. It clung flatteringly to her waist and flowed into a silk swirl around her ankles.

The two girls entered the building through a carved stone entranceway, then paused to look around at the large, airy main room. The abstract paintings on the walls provided a pleasant contrast to the flowery, ornate style of the old stone building in which the gala was being held.

"Mmm," Bess said, eyeing the sumptuous buffet that stretched along one wall. "I'm starved!"

"You'd better eat fast," Nancy warned. "You have to leave in an hour to take your watch post."

Nancy spotted Claudia with Sandro and Massimo. Both guys looked elegant in their tuxedos. Claudia wore a black dress shot with gold thread, and her hair was swept up in a glossy black bun. After Nancy and Bess had each taken a plate full of food, they went over to join the others.

"Where's Karine?" Bess asked Massimo, eyeing the crowd. Except for their group, most of the people seemed to be older society types.

"She is with her father somewhere," Massimo replied. "Over there."

Several yards away, Karine was standing with a portly man. Nancy got only a glimpse of him before he turned to talk to someone else. At the same time Karine caught sight of Nancy's group and headed over to join them.

Continuing to let her eyes wander, Nancy spotted Paola Rinzini across the room, and then Sandro's mother laughing loudly with friends at a table. Nancy was just beginning to wonder where Signor Andreotti was when he made his grand entrance into the room.

The art dealer was wearing a tuxedo, and he had a tall, blond woman on his arm. She was dressed in a gold jumpsuit with a strapless top. A gorgeous gold Etruscan necklace rested on her collarbone, catching the light in the room like a carved jewel.

Signor Andreotti was as good as his word, Nancy thought with satisfaction. No one in the room could miss that necklace or resist it.

"Look at that woman," Karine said as she

stepped up to the group. "I didn't know Signor Andreotti had an *amóre!*"

"She certainly is stunning," Claudia commented. "What a gorgeous outfit!"

"And the necklace. It is almost blinding," Massimo said with appreciation.

"They're coming this way," Nancy said, noting his interest. "Maybe we'll get a chance to see it up close."

Just as Nancy had arranged, Signor Andreotti came over to the group and introduced his date, Alexa Pierre. Massimo admired her necklace openly. Each bead had its own scene, created painstakingly from the placement of tiny points of gold.

"Fabio gave it to me," Alexa told Massimo, a French accent coloring her words. "It's very expensive."

"But beautiful on her, don't you think?" Signor Andreotti put in. "After the party I'm going to show her off in the streets of Rome."

"I couldn't possibly wear this in the streets, darling," Alexa protested. "It is too valuable. Someone would steal it."

Signor Andreotti laughed. "I'll protect you."

Alexa shook her head. "I will leave it in the hotel room," she said, as if making the decision on the spur of the moment. "It will be safer there."

The conversation set up the trap perfectly, Nancy thought, exactly as they had planned.

"Where are you staying?" Nancy asked, as if she didn't already know.

"The Belvedere," Alexa told them. "On the top floor, overlooking the Colosseum."

A few moments later a smiling Signor Andreotti swept his date away. Nancy watched as he moved to another cluster of people to plant his story.

Glancing at her watch, Nancy saw that it was a quarter to nine. Time for the next phase of their plan. A few minutes later Bess excused herself to go to the ladies' room and asked Nancy to join her.

"Signor Andreotti told his friend at the hotel that I'd be there at nine," she said once they were in the empty lounge. "Tell me again—which one of the Belvedere's elevators is the express."

"The one on the right," Nancy reminded her. "The thief will have to take it to get to Alexa's room and to get out of the hotel after he tries to steal the necklace."

"I don't have to tackle anyone, right?" Bess asked anxiously. "I'd hate to be trapped with someone bigger than me."

"All you have to do is see his face," Nancy said. "Don't worry. As soon as Alexa and Signor Andreotti leave, I'll leave, too. I'll be waiting in the hotel room to surprise the thief, and Signor Andreotti will be guarding the stairwell. You won't be alone."

Nancy returned to the gala, telling her friends that Bess was feeling sick and had taken a cab back to the hotel. By now a band was playing, and everyone was so busy dancing that they didn't question Nancy's explanation.

As the clock struck nine-thirty Signor Andreotti gave Nancy a signal and quietly left the room with his date. Nancy gave him five minutes, then excused herself. Jumping on her Vespa, she headed for the Belvedere Hotel.

The Belvedere lobby was small but filled with mirrors and plants. The reception desk was on the left, and two elevators stood in the middle of the room. One went to the bottom four floors and the other was an express to the suites on the top two floors. Signor Andreotti was positioned at the bottom of the fire stairs in an alcove at the rear of the space, out of sight of most of the lobby. If the thief bypassed the elevators, the art dealer would see him or her on the stairs.

Nancy got into the express elevator on the right and asked the operator for the top floor.

As the door closed the elevator operator turned to Nancy and asked, "Well, how do I look?"

It was Bess. She was wearing a black elevator operator's costume, complete with a short frilly skirt and a small round cap. Beneath the cap she had on a black curly wig she and Nancy had bought the day before. Wire-rimmed glasses completed the disguise. Nancy hardly recognized her.

"So far everything's been fine," Bess went on, giggling nervously. "I'm just glad no one has said anything to me. Otherwise they'd know in a second that I don't speak Italian."

"You're perfect," Nancy said as they reached the top floor and she got out. "See you soon!"

Nancy knocked on the door to the north suite, and Alexa Pierre let her in. She had changed into slacks and a tank top and had taken her hair down. Stepping inside, Nancy found herself in a plush sitting room. A door on the right led to the bedroom. The large balcony spanned both rooms and looked out over the Colosseum.

"You're a very good actress," Nancy told Alexa. "I'm sure it's tough to get all that information into a conversation and still make it sound natural."

The blond woman laughed. "Actually, my only worry was that someone would rip this off my neck," she said. "I am glad I do not have to feel responsible anymore." She took off the necklace, then slipped it into a velvet bag and handed the bag to Nancy.

"Your clothes are on the bed," Alexa added. "I'm off to the café to wait for Fabio. I don't want to be here if anyone does break in. I hope you'll be very careful."

Nancy promised she would be. Once she was alone she went into the bedroom and closed the door. She put the velvet bag in the top drawer of the nightstand. Then she slipped into the black turtleneck and stirrup pants she had brought over from the pensione. After lacing up her black sneakers, she looked in the bedroom mirror. The dark clothes would make it difficult for the thief to see her. She gave her reflection a satisfied nod, then slipped out through the French doors onto the balcony.

A full moon hung over Rome, bathing the city in a gentle white light. A band played somewhere in the distance. Nancy was leaning against the side of the building, enjoying the evening air, when she heard a knock on the door. Instantly alert, she crouched down next to the double doors. Through the windows of the French doors she had a perfect view of the bedroom.

After a few moments the door to the bedroom opened, and a tall silhouette stood in the doorway between the two rooms. It was a man dressed in black, wearing a ski mask. He tiptoed over to the bathroom and looked inside. Then he began to search the room.

It didn't take long before he opened the nightstand drawer and took out the velvet bag. As he did, Nancy opened the balcony doors and stepped into the room.

"Stop where you are," she said. "The police are downstairs."

The thief froze for a minute, then broke for the door. Nancy grabbed him, trying to throw him off balance, but he managed to pull away. She then launched a karate kick. The man nimbly jumped to the side, then grabbed Nancy's arms.

Nancy struggled to break free enough to reach his mask. She didn't have to overpower him, she told herself. She only had to see his face.

Suddenly the thief shoved Nancy backward into the dresser. She tumbled, hitting her knee as she fell. Sharp pain shot through her, slowing her down for a moment.

Before she could get up the man stuffed the velvet bag into his pocket and dashed into the living room, swinging the door between the two rooms closed behind him. Springing to her feet, Nancy grabbed the handle. She was locked in!

Chapter

Twelve

NANCY HEARD THE suite's outside door slam. Desperately she tugged at the bedroom door again, but it didn't budge. He was getting away!

The balcony! she suddenly remembered. It opened off both rooms. She raced outside, flung open the balcony doors to the living room, then ran for the suite's outside door.

The hall was empty, but there was a clatter in the stairwell. She had told the thief that the police were downstairs, Nancy remembered. He probably didn't trust the elevator.

As quickly as her painful knee would let her, Nancy ran to the stairs. The thief was about one floor below, swinging downward as fast as he could. She could hear him, and occasionally she caught a glimpse of his ski mask. But she knew she wasn't going to be able to catch him.

The lobby door closed with a bang as Nancy rounded the last flight of stairs. She slammed the door open as she went through after him.

The place was in an uproar. Signor Andreotti was sitting on the floor, his face red. "He went that way!" he yelled, pointing at the main door.

Nancy paused, torn between following the thief and helping Signor Andreotti.

"Don't worry about me, I'm fine," he roared, seeing her indecision. "Get that little *cretino!*"

Nancy ran outside in time to see the thief leap onto a dark-colored Vespa in front of the hotel. A silver decal flashed as he swung his leg over the motor scooter. She ran for her own Vespa, reaching it just as he squealed away.

Nancy's engine roared to life, and she was after him, racing through the streets. He turned onto a cobblestone road, trying to lose her on the twists and turns. She followed closely, but he was weaving so much that she didn't know which turns he was taking until she was almost on them.

Looking behind him to see where Nancy was, the thief took a turn too tightly. The Vespa hit the corner of a building and smashed its taillight. He wavered for a minute, then regained his balance in time to make another quick turn, to the left.

Nancy followed him and found herself in a tiny piazza. Roads ran off to her right and left, but the dark Vespa was nowhere in sight. She could hear the engine, but the sound bounced around the piazza, and she couldn't tell where it was coming from. She had lost him.

Nancy's knee ached. Sighing in frustration, she drove back slowly to the Belvedere. Bess and Signor Andreotti were gone, but there was a message from Bess saying she'd gone back to their pensione. When Nancy got back, Bess was waiting up for her.

"From the look on your face, your news is as bad as mine," Bess said.

Nancy sank into the overstuffed chair. "You didn't see him, then?" she asked.

Bess shook her head. "I took a few families up to the top floor, and several couples came down. But I didn't see any guy on his own. And Signor Andreotti didn't get a look at him, either. The guy totally bowled him over."

"I feel awful about losing that necklace," Nancy said, resting her chin in her hands. "The thief must have taken the other elevator and walked up the last two flights. I guess I should have called the police. I was just sure that one of us would see his face!"

"So we don't know any more now than we did before," Bess mused.

"Well, we know the thief is a young man," Nancy said. "And he has a dark-colored Vespa, with a silver decal on the side. He busted his taillight trying to get away from me, too."

"Not to mention that he was at the party tonight," Bess added. "That narrows it down."

"To Massimo, Sandro, and a few others," Nancy said. "I guess we know what we're doing in the morning—trying to match dark Vespas with people who were at the party."

"Not first thing," Bess said, shooting Nancy a secretive smile. "I have a little surprise first."

Nancy looked at Bess questioningly. "What?"

"You have to wait until morning," Bess said mysteriously. "I promise you it's a good surprise."

"Okay, Bess," Nancy said the next morning, casting one last glance in the mirror at the sleeveless white blouse and flowered shorts she wore. "What's the big secret? I can't wait anymore."

Bess only said, "All in good time." Nancy was dying of curiosity as Bess led her to the outdoor café down the block. Bess murmured something to the waiter, and Nancy was surprised when he showed them to a table where someone else was already sitting. A blond guy was there, turned away from them so that Nancy could see only his profile and dark glasses.

Then he turned his head and slipped the glasses off his nose. It was Mick Devlin!

A smile spread slowly across his handsome face as he watched Nancy come toward him. Then he stood up, opened his arms, and scooped her into them, hugging her tightly.

"Mick," Nancy gasped, pulling away. Her heart was pounding wildly. "What are you doing here?"

"I came to do this," he said. His eyes held her as he curled one hand around the back of her neck and covered her mouth in a kiss that seemed to go on forever.

Bess noisily cleared her throat. "If I had known you'd get so lost in each other, I wouldn't have come along!" she teased.

Nancy blushed and untangled herself. She smoothed her hair, then took the chair next to Mick, while Bess sat on his other side.

"So really," she said, composing herself, "what are you doing here?"

Just then their waiter came over to take their order. Mick waited until he was gone before answering Nancy's question. "Really, I came to see you." He couldn't seem to stop smiling. "I was tired of Geneva, and I missed you guys."

Nancy was still feeling stunned. "But how did you find us?"

"I remembered Claudia's name, so I called her up. Don't worry, no strings attached," Mick added quickly. "But we had a good time in Geneva, right? And we made a good team while you were solving your mystery."

"Well, we've stumbled into another one," Bess told him. "Funny how that happens when Nancy's around. Maybe you can help us with this one, too."

Over pastries and fruit Nancy and Bess filled Mick in on the events of the past week. Nancy could hardly keep her mind on what she was saying—her heart skipped a beat every time Mick smiled.

When she was done, Mick took her hand in his and fixed her with his deep green eyes. "Looks like I have a lot of lost time to make up for," he said. "And a few bumps on the head that someone needs to pay for. What's your next step? Are you going to see this Massimo character?"

Nancy nodded. "And call Signor Andreotti to make sure he's okay."

"Well, we might be wrapping up this mystery any second," Bess pointed out. "Maybe we should wait until we have some news for him."

"Massimo first, then," Mick said, signaling for the waiter. "And I hope you won't mind if I come along for the ride."

Nancy returned Mick's grin and caught Bess looking at her. Romance was the best part of life to Bess, Nancy knew, regardless of whose romance it was. And right now, Nancy had to agree!

The teenagers unlocked their Vespas and set off for Piazza Navona, with Mick riding behind Nancy. Feeling Mick's arms wrapped loosely around her, Nancy resisted the urge to lean her head back into his shoulder. Get a grip on yourself, Drew, she told herself sternly. Yesterday you had written this guy off. Today the least you can do is keep your head long enough to catch the jewelry thief.

The two Vespas buzzed down to Piazza Navona. Nancy spotted Massimo right away. He was sitting on his stool, watching the tourists.

"I'll take Mick over and introduce him," Bess offered after the girls had parked their Vespas. "Kind of a diversion, you know. That way you can look around for Massimo's Vespa."

Mick gave Nancy a thumbs-up sign. "She's separating us already," he joked, heading toward the jewelry stand.

Nancy nosed around in the rack of motor scooters, looking for Massimo's. She had no trouble identifying the black Vespa by the license plate, which read Bianco 1. The Vespa was dirty, but even as she rubbed the dirt from the body she couldn't find any trace of a decal. Then she checked the taillight. It was intact and very dirty, Nancy saw. This definitely wasn't the Vespa she had chased the night before.

The sound of another Vespa motor made Nancy look up. Claudia was just pulling up on her moped. Bluish circles under her eyes clearly showed her lack of sleep. She looked upset.

"I have to talk to you," she told Nancy, not even bothering to say hello. "I have some news."

"If you tracked us here, it must be important."

"Actually, you were gone, so I was coming to see Massimo." Claudia paused and gazed at the jewelry stand. She didn't seem to know how to begin.

"I have some news, too," Nancy said. "We set a trap for the thief last night, but he got away."

Claudia didn't look surprised. "What happened?" she asked.

Briefly Nancy told her about the trap and the chase through the streets. "I thought it was Massimo, but his Vespa isn't the one that the thief was riding," she concluded.

Claudia gave a half nod. "Is that Mick Devlin with Bess?" she asked, changing the subject. Nancy turned and saw Bess and Mick heading back their way.

"Yes," Nancy replied. "I heard he called you to find us. Thanks for keeping his call a secret. I was really surprised."

A cloud crossed Claudia's face as Nancy said the

word *secret*. She greeted Bess and gave Mick two air kisses, then turned back to Nancy. "I want to show you something," she said, getting back on her Vespa. "Follow me."

Nancy exchanged puzzled looks with Bess and Mick. They all got on their bikes and rode away from the square, with Claudia out in front. Soon Nancy recognized the route Claudia was taking. Within minutes they rode up the ramp of the Theater of Marcellus and pulled into the parking lot.

The first thing Nancy saw was a midnight blue Vespa next to where Claudia had parked. The taillight was broken. Nancy ran her hand over the seat as she walked around it. A shiny decal on the body proclaimed *Roma* in silver letters.

"This is it!" she said excitedly, digging in her purse to write down the license plate number. "Claudia, you're brilliant!"

Nancy pulled out a piece of paper and started to write, but Claudia stopped her.

"There is no need for that," Claudia said.

"What do you mean?" Nancy asked, looking up.

A tear trickled down Claudia's cheek, and she spoke so softly that Nancy could hardly hear her. "The bike belongs to Sandro."

Chapter
Thirteen

Hᴏᴡ ʟᴏɴɢ ʜᴀᴠᴇ you known?" Nancy asked.

Claudia wiped away her tears with the back of her hand. "I have suspected it since the night at the disco. Massimo was so offended when we suggested the necklace had come from him," she said slowly. "We have been friends since we were children, and I knew he would not lie about something like that. Then there was the part about Sandro forgetting to bring the package to the store for over a week. That is not like him at all. Especially since when he dropped off the package, he said it was very important."

So that was why Claudia had been so upset. She was afraid of finding out her boyfriend was a jewelry thief! "Why didn't you tell us that Sandro's story seemed strange to you?" Nancy asked.

"Well, I was uncertain. So when Massimo and I

were dancing, I asked him point-blank. 'Did you give a package to Sandro?' I asked. 'How many necklaces were in it?' "

"How many?" Bess breathed.

"Two," Claudia said.

"But Sandro gave you a package with *three* necklaces," Nancy said. "I still don't understand why you didn't say something right away."

Claudia fingered the seat of her Vespa as she answered. "It was Sandro against Massimo. I did not know who was lying. And they are both so dear to me, I could not risk making a mistake."

"So when were you sure?" Bess prodded.

"Last night," Claudia replied. "Sandro and I planned to go out after the party, but he canceled. He just said he had something else to do. He even left his mother at the opening. I took her home and waited at his house for a while, but he never showed up. When I finally left, I ran into him pulling into the parking lot. He was dressed all in black, and he was very tense and upset."

There was no doubt in Nancy's mind. Sandro was their thief. But something else still bothered her. "Why would he do it?" she asked.

"Steal from his mother?" Claudia asked bitterly. "Attack my friends? We will have to ask him."

Nancy's mind was working furiously as the foursome went upstairs. Thinking back, she was pretty sure she knew why Sandro had stolen the necklaces, but there were still a few blanks.

"Claudia, what are you doing here?" Sandro asked, bending to kiss her as he invited the four teens inside.

Stiffly, Claudia introduced Mick and Sandro, then looked around. "Is your mother here?" she asked.

"She's out shopping," he said, following the group into the living room. "What's going on?"

"Why did you do it, Sandro?" Claudia stared him straight in the eyes. "Why did you steal your own mother's necklace? And her friends' jewelry?"

Sandro looked innocently from Claudia to Nancy, opening his palms in front of him. "Is this a joke?" he asked. "What are you talking about?"

"Those women trusted you!" Claudia continued. "You probably stole their jewelry from their homes when you were an invited guest!"

"Claudia"—Sandro gave an uneasy laugh—"you're acting crazy. I'm not a thief."

"If you lie to me again, I will never speak to you as long as I live." Claudia's voice shook. "I saw you last night, and so did Nancy!"

Sandro's face crumpled. He sat down heavily on the sofa.

"Let me see if I have the story right," Nancy said, sitting down next to him. "You steal the jewelry and send it to Preziosi. Paola sells it."

"But why?" Claudia asked, her lips tight. She sat down on Sandro's other side while Mick and Bess settled into two chairs.

"Because he wants to start his own computer company and his mother wouldn't lend him the money," Nancy guessed. Sandro's astonished expression told her she was right. "But then why haven't you started the company?"

Bess grabbed Nancy's arm. "Wait, I'm completely lost!" she exclaimed. "Could you guys please back up and explain this to me?"

"Nancy's right," Sandro said miserably, raking a hand through his hair. "I took my mother's necklace so I could start my own company. But I only wanted to borrow it," he added earnestly. "I thought I could pawn it, but I needed to be sure I would be able to get it back as soon as the company made some money. I was hoping my mother wouldn't miss it. She almost never wears it."

Sandro let out a sigh before continuing. "One day I was at Preziosi, waiting for Claudia to come back from an errand, and I asked Paola to recommend a pawnshop. She got the story out of me and offered to lend me the money herself—in exchange for the necklace."

"How were you going to explain where you got the money to open your business?" Bess asked, leaning forward in her chair.

"I wasn't sure," Sandro admitted. "As it turned out, it didn't matter because Paola didn't give me any money. She kept Mamma's necklace and blackmailed me into stealing again instead. She said if I didn't, she'd tell my mother I stole her necklace. She said that no one would believe I really intended to get it back for her."

"But how did you manage to steal everyone's jewelry?" Bess asked.

"As Claudia said, I was invited into all those houses," Sandro said. "You can't believe how careless some people are with their combinations.

And I have a listening device so I can hear the combination in the locks. It was pretty easy."

Nancy picked up the story again. "So when you met Bess on the Spanish Steps, you must have recognized the necklace she was wearing right away. When the gypsy kids grabbed her knapsack, you saw your chance to grab her necklace."

"But I managed to hold on to it," Bess put in. "That's why we didn't suspect you then."

Pointing an accusing finger at Sandro, Claudia said, "You drugged Nancy at the disco and broke into their room twice."

Sandro nodded, looking ashamed. "I picked up Bess's room key when the kids took her knapsack, so I knew where to go." He smiled sheepishly. "The second time I wore a wig that was kind of like Massimo's hair. I thought that would give you more reason to suspect him."

"Where did you get that awful gargoyle's head?" Bess asked.

"At an art supply store," said Sandro. "I hoped that would make you think of Massimo, too."

Nancy shuddered as she remembered the attack in the catacombs and the musty bones crashing around her. "That was quite a daring move in the catacombs," she told Sandro. "I don't know if I would have had the guts to attack someone with all my friends around."

"I had to," Sandro said. "Paola promised me if I could only get the necklace back, I could stop stealing for her."

The group fell silent for a moment until Sandro spoke. "I guess I should be happy," he said, despair in his voice. "I've been trying to get out of this for months. I'm sorry I hurt you, Nancy. I was just so desperate. I tried to warn you, but you wouldn't give up!"

Tears sprang to Claudia's eyes, and Bess went over to hug her.

"I know you were scared," Nancy told Sandro. "But you stole a lot of jewelry. Why didn't you simply go to the police and report Paola?"

"I don't have any proof," Sandro said. "Paola made that very clear. She said she would put the blame on me and send me to jail!"

Claudia's dark eyes flashed with indignation. "There must be some way to catch her," she said.

"Red-handed is always the best way," Nancy said with a smile. "All we have to do is catch Paola with the goods."

For the first time since they had confronted Sandro, Mick spoke up. "So you need a stolen necklace," he said. "Do you have one?"

"I have the necklace I took from the hotel last night," Sandro said. "And I still have the one I took from Nancy in the catacombs. You mean I can just give them to Paola and have her arrested?" he asked, his expression brightening.

Nancy's mind was racing. "Not quite," she said. "We'd have to prove she knew they were stolen and kept them anyway. The best thing would be if we could catch her trying to sell them."

"They are not sold in the store," Claudia said, looking at Sandro. "Who does she sell them to?"

Sandro shrugged, "If she told me that, she would be a real fool."

Nancy wasn't about to give up, though. She was sure they were on the right track. "But if she has them to sell, I'll bet we could find out who her contact is," she pointed out.

"Let's track her!" Mick suggested.

Sandro looked at Nancy, his eyes wide. "You mean, you're letting me off the hook? You're not going to turn me over to the police?"

"Not at the moment," Nancy said. "We need you to get to Paola. But you'll have to talk to the police once we've caught her."

"Claudia, I'm so terribly sorry," Sandro said, hugging her tightly. "If I get out of this, I promise I'll never be so stupid again."

Nancy waited for the couple to separate, then said, "Claudia, maybe you should go to Preziosi to see if Paola is there. Sandro can take the necklaces over in a little while."

Claudia grimaced and said, "I am already late for work, so I should go there, anyway."

"Since she forced me to break into that hotel last night, she's probably expecting me," Sandro put in. "I'm supposed to go to work, but I can tell them I'm not coming."

"That won't be necessary," Nancy said as an idea came to her. "You can tell Paola you're sending the necklaces over with a friend. Claudia, you watch her to see if she tries to arrange a meeting with anyone."

"But who will bring the necklaces to the store?" Claudia asked Nancy. "Neither you nor Bess can do it. Paola would suspect something right away."

Nancy had already thought of that. "Mick will

take them, and I'll follow him. That way, if she leaves the store, we can tail her."

The plan went perfectly. Paola was at the store when Sandro called to let her know his "messenger" would deliver the necklaces. A few minutes later Mick was on his way. Nancy and Bess followed him, waiting for him at a café across the street from Preziosi.

"She barely glanced at me," Mick said when he joined them. "She just took the package and slipped it directly into her shoulder bag."

Nancy, Mick, and Bess hung around the café for an hour, waiting for Paola to make a move. Nancy was glad to hear about what Mick had been up to the last several weeks, but she deliberately steered the conversation away from herself. She didn't want to have to think about what his trip to Rome meant for them yet—at least not until they had Paola safely behind bars.

Finally, just before lunch, Paola left the store. Bess went back into Preziosi to see if Claudia had learned anything special, while Nancy and Mick followed Paola. They barely squeezed onto the bus she had boarded in time.

Luckily for Nancy, the bus was packed. She couldn't even get to the ticket punch to stamp her ticket. She hid her face in Mick's shoulder, praying Paola wouldn't see her.

Paola didn't even look around. She got off at Piazza Navona and strolled through the crowds of tourists. The piazza was packed with people, so it was easy for Nancy and Mick to avoid being seen.

The only trouble was, it could also be easy for Paola to lose them.

But Paola's attention was on the artists, not the crowd. She was making her way slowly toward Massimo's stand. Was she going to meet him after all? Nancy wondered as they followed several yards behind her.

Nancy didn't see Massimo near his stand. Apparently Paola didn't either. She slowed her pace but passed the stand without stopping. She seemed to be headed toward something else.

The gallery owner was looking at a chalk drawing. Nancy recognized the petite, dark-haired artist who was half lying on the ground, scratching intensely at the pavement with her chalk. It was Karine. Massimo was sitting cross-legged on the ground, watching her work.

Paola said something to Karine, and the girl looked up for a moment. Karine smiled briefly before returning to her work. Paola dropped a few coins in a cup near Karine and continued on, looking at a few of the craft stands.

"Parla Deutsch?" Someone near Nancy was calling out in hopelessly mangled Italian. Nancy turned and saw a family looking lost and a little desperate.

"Ah, Nancy?" Mick called from behind her. The family had grabbed him, and a torrent of German swirled around him.

"They want directions, I think," he said, an apologetic look on his face. "I think I can make out what they're saying, but I don't know my way around this place."

Nancy looked through the crowd for Paola. "Mick, we have to go," she said, trying for a polite smile. "Tell them you don't know."

Mick tried to explain, but the father of the family wouldn't release his arm.

"Come on, Mick," Nancy urged.

Mick pulled free and headed after Nancy, but it was too late. Paola had disappeared!

Chapter

Fourteen

NANCY'S HEART FELL. "I don't see her anywhere."

"Do you think she stopped to get something to eat?" Mick suggested.

"I'm sure she's meeting someone," she said with a frustrated sigh. "But it's weird—she didn't seem to be looking for anyone. She didn't even look around on her way here to see if she was being followed."

"If her contact isn't here, why come at all?" Mick asked, looking puzzled.

Good question, Nancy thought. "Maybe she was waiting for some sort of signal," she suggested.

"A signal we missed," Mick said, grimacing. "Thanks to those tourists."

In her mind Nancy played over everything they had seen Paola do. "Wait a minute," she said.

"Maybe one of the artists tipped her off. Let's find out."

Karine was still hard at work, her dark hair hanging over her face as she concentrated on her chalk sketch. As Nancy and Mick approached Massimo greeted them from where he was sitting.

"You have come to see Karine's work?" Massimo asked.

"We've been so busy that we haven't had a chance before," Nancy said politely. "It's really beautiful, isn't it?"

"These drawings take hours." Massimo watched Karine's broad strokes with approval.

"Karine," Nancy began, trying not to be too abrupt. "Paola Rinzini was just here. She stopped to see your drawing. Did she say anything to you?"

Karine didn't bother to look up. "Just what she always says. 'Nice work,' or something like that."

It seemed odd to Nancy that someone as sophisticated and self-absorbed as Paola would come all the way to Piazza Navona simply to compliment Karine on her work.

What she always says, Nancy mentally repeated Karine's words. Gazing at the sketch, she saw that it was a copy of one of Michelangelo's greatest works, *The Creation of Adam,* which he had painted on the ceiling of the Sistine Chapel.

Could Karine's artwork be a clue? Nancy wondered.

"Well, Paola's right, it's beautiful. And I'm glad we came by to see it," Nancy said sincerely. "How did you decide what to draw today?"

"My father suggested it this morning," Karine said, still bent over her work.

That strange request again, Nancy thought. Why would Karine's father want her to draw something that he never came to see? But *Paola* had come to see it, she realized.

Nancy's heart leapt. Karine's father was an import-export trader, she remembered. That was a perfect business for smuggling jewelry out of the country. He could be Paola's contact!

"Let's go," she said in a low voice, practically dragging Mick away. "I know where Paola is going."

Calling a hasty goodbye to Massimo and Karine, Mick and Nancy ran into the street, trying to hail a cab.

"Where are we going?" Mick wanted to know.

"To the Vatican Museums," Nancy said. "I'll explain on the way. You could say I just got a divine message!"

"Which way is the Sistine Chapel?" Nancy asked urgently as she and Mick bought tickets at the museum entrance.

The ticket seller frowned at Nancy's impatience. "We have signs posted with directions in every language," he told her.

Moving into the museum, Nancy saw that the ticket seller was right: There were four different tours, organized according to time. Their routes were coded neatly by color on diagrams posted inside the entrance.

Not wanting to lose a minute, Nancy and Mick

picked the shortest route, which led almost directly to the Sistine Chapel. They hurried up the wide
marble stairway into a hall that sloped gently
downward. The hall seemed almost endless.

Searching left and right for Paola, Nancy and
Mick dashed down the hall. Their roving eyes
passed over huge woven tapestries and glass cases
full of handwritten Bibles lettered in gold. On one
side tall windows stood open, letting a breeze flow
into the museum. Through them Nancy could see
the Vatican gardens below. Perfect geometric flow-
er beds looked as if they had been cut out with a
pair of scissors—but no Paola.

When they finally reached the end of the hallway, they took a sharp turn and found themselves
in the first of a series of rooms that had been
painted by the artist Raphael.

The rooms were small and quite dark. Limited
light filtered in through tiny windows. Nancy
blinked, letting her eyes adjust to the gloom. The
walls and ceilings were painted in rich colors.
Scenes of old Rome and stories from the Bible
stretched out before them, displaying figures bigger than life.

The masterworks had drawn a crowd of art
students, who looked up at the pair's noisy intru-
sion. Nancy and Mick slowed to a fast walk, trying
to look like eager tourists.

"Where is it?" Mick asked impatiently, striding
through the rooms a few steps in front of Nancy.

She looked past Mick's shoulders to the series of
doors ahead. There was Paola Rinzini, wandering
through the room directly in front of them!

Nancy grabbed Mick's arm, making him yelp in surprise. "Ow," he said, turning around. Mick's protest had caught the attention of a few tourists. "Why are you stopping? Aren't we in a hurry?"

"She's here," Nancy hissed, pulling Mick into a corner. "Paola's in the next room."

A short man with brilliant green eyes looked over at them. He must be a businessman on his lunch hour, Nancy thought, noting his double-breasted suit. He looked vaguely familiar. She smiled blankly at him until he turned back to the painting he'd been admiring.

"Do you know him?" Mick whispered.

Nancy shook her head. "I thought so. But I can't place him. He must remind me of someone."

Cautiously Nancy and Mick entered the next room. It was the last of the Raphael rooms. Paola was nowhere in sight. Nancy realized that the woman had gone right into the Sistine Chapel.

Mick surveyed the winding hallway leading into the chapel. "She'll see us the minute we step over the threshold," he pointed out.

"Not if we go in with a lot of people," Nancy said, her eyes on a group of students approaching. Mick caught up with a tall, black-haired girl in the group. Nancy followed behind him, letting Mick's broad shoulders block her from sight. Footsteps and shuffling were the only noises in the room.

Admiring tourists crowded the chapel, covering Nancy and Mick's entrance. Guards posted at every door warned the visitors to talk quietly and not to use the flash equipment on their cameras.

Overhearing the students' guide, Nancy learned that the Sistine Chapel was one of Michelangelo's most awe-inspiring masterpieces. He had spent more than four years lying on his back, painting the scenes from the Bible's Old Testament that graced the ceiling. Then he had turned his energy to the wall behind the altar and created *The Last Judgment,* the forty-five-foot fresco that dominated the room.

As she listened Nancy searched out Paola. She was standing in front of a sign that explained the fresco technique.

"Miss! Miss!" A man's booming voice broke the silence. Nancy jumped. He was speaking English.

The security guards immediately shushed him, but he ignored them.

"Miss, is this yours?" he called again. This time Nancy detected a trace of an accent, although she couldn't tell from where.

The security guards left their posts at the doors, elbowing their way through the tourists. They were coming toward their group, Nancy realized. She tried to duck behind Mick. Why did they have to be coming this way? she thought.

"Miss!" the man repeated insistently. "You, with the red hair!"

He couldn't mean me, Nancy thought in panic. But he was walking straight for her. It was the short, pudgy businessman she'd seen earlier, she realized. The one with the brilliant green eyes.

Worse yet, his yelling had drawn Paola's attention. She saw Nancy and froze for a moment, her eyes darting between Nancy and the man who was approaching her. Turning on her heel, she fled the room, leaving Nancy watching helplessly.

We've really lost her this time, Nancy thought. The security guards and the man with the brilliant eyes were almost upon her.

"Silènzio!" one of the guards ordered, grabbing the businessman's arm. Then, to her astonishment, the man grabbed Nancy!

"Silènzio, Signore!" the guard demanded again.

With his hand still on Nancy's arm the green-eyed man turned to the guard and spoke to him in a low voice. They argued briefly in Italian. Finally the guards moved off after receiving assurances that the man wouldn't cause trouble again.

"They certainly are touchy, aren't they?" the man asked Nancy in a normal tone. For the first time he seemed to notice that he was holding Nancy's arm, and he released her immediately. "Is this yours?"

He held out a small green guidebook. "I saw you running through the rooms back there and figured you must have been the one to drop it."

"No, it's not ours," Mick answered for Nancy, his eyes flashing angrily.

"I was sure it was," the man said. "You were in such a hurry."

Nancy looked at the book. It was a tourist's guide to Italy—but written in French!

Suspicious, Nancy asked the man, "How did you guess we spoke English? This book is in French."

"Oh, well," he said smoothly, "English is the language of tourists, isn't it? And you look American. At least your friend here does." He gestured to Mick.

"Then why would we drop a *French* guidebook?" Nancy pressed.

"I'm sorry!" the man said, throwing his hands in the air. He looked offended. "I was only trying to help." He shrugged and walked away, swinging the guidebook in his hand.

Mick was fuming. "We almost had her, and some Good Samaritan had to bungle the whole thing!"

"That was no Good Samaritan," Nancy said grimly. Suddenly she realized where she'd seen those green eyes before. "That was Mr. Azar— Karine's father!"

Chapter
Fifteen

KARINE'S THE ONE who made the chalk drawing, right?" Mick asked.

Seeing his confused expression, Nancy remembered that he wasn't as familiar with this case as she was. "Right, and her father asked her to draw it," she explained. "That must be how he let Paola know where to meet him."

Mick whistled softly. "You mean, he's Paola's contact? But why didn't he just call her?"

"Phones can be bugged, and calls leave records. No one could trace him through a chalk drawing."

"You've cracked the case!" Mick burst out, swinging her around in a circle. "Let's call the police and have them round up the criminals!"

Nancy smiled at his enthusiasm. "We don't have any proof," she pointed out. "All Karine's father did was try to return a guidebook."

"He'll have to try again to get the necklace from

Paola," Mick said, nodding. "Next time we can have the police there."

Nancy wished it were that easy. "We'll never have time to tip off the police unless we know in advance when and where she's meeting him," she said. "Even with police help we can't just watch them both twenty-four hours a day. Besides, they're going to be much more careful now to make sure they aren't followed."

Nancy and Mick found a telephone and called Preziosi to tell Claudia and Bess what had happened. Nancy described the green-eyed man carefully, and Claudia confirmed her guess.

"That sounds like Mr. Azar," Claudia said. "Is Karine in on this, too? I am surrounded by criminals!"

"She could be, but I don't think so. She wouldn't have told us her father requested the painting if she was. There's a good chance Mr. Azar doesn't even realize we figured out his secret signal," Nancy said, thinking aloud. "He probably thinks we just followed Paola from the store. I bet he'll use Karine's drawing again for their next rendezvous. His system has been foolproof so far."

Claudia's frustrated voice wailed back over the line. "But he could wait for days!"

"I think he'll move right away," Nancy told her, "and we'll have to be ready for him when he does. Even if they use the drawing again, Paola and Mr. Azar need to fix a rendezvous time, so stay by the phone and tell Bess to follow Paola if she has to."

"What if Paola goes home instead of coming

here?" Claudia asked. "Should I call Sandro and ask him to cover her apartment?"

Nancy thought for a moment. "No. Mr. Azar is worried about being connected to Paola, and trying her at the store is less risky. Just watch her, Claudia. We're on our way back to that café across the street." Saying goodbye, Nancy hung up.

Bess was pacing around outside the café when Nancy and Mick returned to via Condotti.

"Paola's back," Bess reported. "And boy, is she in a foul mood! When she saw me she said I was bothering her employees and practically shoved me out the door."

"Did she say anything about seeing Nancy and me at the Sistine Chapel?" Mick asked.

Bess shook her head. "And I'm sure she would have, if she thought you guys were just sightseeing. She definitely knows we're on to her."

"Claudia's been camped out near the phone in the front since you called," Bess went on. "That way she can pick up the extension the minute Paola gets a call in her office."

Nancy, Bess, and Mick hovered near the café's window. They had been there for about two hours when Claudia burst out of the store and ran over.

"She got a call!" Claudia exclaimed. "I am almost sure it was Mr. Azar. A man's voice said, 'Four forty-five tomorrow. Come alone this time.' He hung up quickly, but I heard traffic noise in the background. He must have called from a pay phone so the call could not be easily traced."

A rush of excitement swept over Nancy. "He

didn't mention a place, so he must be relying on Karine's drawing again," she told the others.

"We could go to Piazza Navona early tomorrow morning and just ask Karine what she's going to draw," Mick suggested. "That way we can be waiting for Paola before she even gets there, so there's no chance of her seeing us follow her."

"Wait a minute," Nancy said. The seed of an idea had just planted itself in her mind. "What if we could get Karine to *change* her drawing? Then we could send Paola wherever we wanted!"

"But we couldn't get Mr. Azar there," Bess pointed out.

Nancy nodded. "Exactly. We can separate them and send the police after Mr. Azar."

"I thought you said we had to catch Paola selling the necklaces," Claudia objected.

"That's true, but we won't be able to catch even one of them red-handed if they see us. And if we blow it again, I'm afraid we won't get another chance," Nancy said soberly.

Mick squeezed Nancy's shoulders, sending a shiver through her. "Besides, if you can catch Paola with the stolen jewelry, she might be willing to testify against Karine's father," he said. "She won't want to take the rap alone."

"So they'll testify against each other!" Bess said triumphantly. "What a great idea. But how do we get Karine to change her drawing?"

"I bet she'd do it for Massimo," Nancy said, raising her eyebrows. "They've been getting very close these last few days. We need a good place for

139

our rendezvous," she continued, her thoughts leaping ahead. "Somewhere Paola won't see us, but not so big that she'll be able to escape."

The teens put their heads together, considering several of Rome's biggest tourist attractions. Finally they settled on the Colosseum.

"It is a huge theater in the round," Claudia told them. "We could surround her easily. And Sandro can rig up some walkie-talkies from his job so we can be in constant contact with one another."

"I want to see it first," Nancy said. "We need to figure out exactly what we're going to do."

"Let me call Sandro and tell him about the walkie-talkies," Claudia said. "He can meet you guys at the Colosseum so you can plan for tomorrow."

The Colosseum was a large oval sports arena more than two thousand years old. In its time it had seated over fifty thousand people. Now it was crumbling. Part of the outside wall had tumbled down, and what remained was marked with layers of arches and holes punched out of the stone by time. It looked like a stone beehive, Nancy thought.

The group walked through the arches and into one of the high tunnels that led to the open arena at the Colosseum's center. The sides sloped up around them, the wooden seats long gone. The original floor of the stadium had rotted away, exposing a maze of stone walls underneath.

"You wouldn't want to slip and fall down there," Sandro warned as they made their way around the edge of the maze where the floor had once been. It was closed off to tourists by a circular railing. He went on to explain that the Romans had stored supplies and animals under the arena floor. There were also tunnels around the sides, which had been used to flood the stadium for water sports.

"This is where the gladiators fought," he told Nancy, Bess, and Mick. "They were slaves thrown together to fight for the entertainment of the masses. The crowds decided their fate."

"What do you mean?" Bess asked.

"When each battle was over, the crowd voted on whether to grant the loser mercy. Thumbs up, he was allowed to live. Thumbs down . . ." Sandro shrugged.

Bess shuddered. "This place is giving me the creeps," she said, eyeing the maze in front of them. "It's not a sports arena, it's a torture chamber!"

The group had walked halfway around the arena floor when Nancy saw a tall gate ahead blocking their path. "It looks like we can't go much farther, anyway," she observed, coming to a stop.

"They don't have enough guards to open the whole place up," Sandro explained as the group headed to the entrance. "They'd have tourists climbing through the tunnels and getting hopelessly lost."

Bess gave a sigh of relief as they left the Colosseum. "I'm going to guard one of the entrances tomorrow," she declared. "I don't want to be anywhere near where the gladiators actually fought. As it is, I'm going to have nightmares for weeks!"

"Massimo convinced Karine to draw the Colosseum," Sandro reported late the following morning when Nancy, Mick, and Bess arrived at his apartment. "Claudia asked him to do it. When she told him it was important, Massimo didn't even ask for an explanation."

According to the plan, Sandro had stopped by Piazza Navona earlier that morning to talk to Karine. When he casually asked about her drawing she told him that her father had asked her to draw the Pantheon. "But she was drawing the Colosseum instead," Sandro confirmed. "She didn't even seem to mind that she was drawing a building, something she usually doesn't do, since she likes colorful drawings."

Nancy felt guilty about using Karine to catch her father, but what could she tell the other girl—that her father was smuggling jewelry and they needed her to capture him?

Claudia was already at Preziosi, Nancy knew. She would call Sandro as soon as Paola left for the Colosseum. That was Sandro and Claudia's cue to call the police and send them to the Pantheon to detain Mr. Azar for questioning. Sandro had also rigged up five walkie-talkies for the group's stakeout at the Colosseum.

The afternoon at Sandro's seemed to drag on forever. By the time the phone rang, a little after four, Nancy was so wound up that she actually jumped in her chair.

"Paola just left," Sandro told them after speaking briefly with Claudia. "She must be headed for Piazza Navona."

The four teenagers raced on the Vespas to the Colosseum to take their positions. Bess watched the street in front of the building while Nancy stood inside the main entrance. Sandro and Mick disappeared inside to keep a lookout from the sides of the Colosseum where the seats used to be.

Since it was late afternoon, there weren't many tourists. Nancy knew that it would have been easier to hide in the midday crowds.

Well, we'll just have to do the best we can, she thought. Claudia would be showing up any minute, and Bess would signal them when she arrived. Claudia was going to watch the side entrance to make sure Paola didn't walk in from there and see them.

By Nancy's calculations they still had about ten minutes before Paola showed up. Each minute seemed to drag on for an eternity. Where was Claudia? Nancy fought down a bubble of unease. Had Paola seen through their trap?

Suddenly Nancy's walkie-talkie crackled. Bess's voice sputtered in and out, and Nancy couldn't make out what she was saying.

"Bess, please repeat," she said urgently. "You're too far away."

Bess's voice broke through the crackling. ". . . Claudia?" Bess's voice cut out and then in again. ". . . she's here," Nancy heard. And then, "Through the front."

Claudia must have arrived, Nancy thought. Bess

was trying to say she was coming to the front, not the side entrance. Paola would probably be there within a few minutes. Nancy had to warn Claudia to get out of sight quickly.

Nancy peered around the corner, keeping her body hidden behind the main arch. No sign of Claudia. Had she gone around to the side after all?

Pressing the talk button, Nancy said, "Where is she, Bess?" As she spoke she stepped out into the doorway so she could hear Bess better. "Do you see her?"

Now Bess's voice came in more clearly. "Nancy, what are you doing?" she asked. "She's right in front of you!"

Nancy looked up. She was face-to-face with Paola Rinzini!

Chapter

Sixteen

NANCY GASPED. How could she have been so careless?

Paola was about fifteen feet away, too far for Nancy to grab her. Nancy's heart sank. If Paola turned and ran out into the street, they'd never get her!

Thinking quickly, Nancy stepped to one side and started to yell. "Oh, no!" she cried, looking behind Paola. "Stop her before she gets inside the Colosseum!" There was a better chance of getting Paola inside the Colosseum if she thought they *didn't* want her there. At least that was what Nancy hoped.

Paola whirled. Bess was racing toward them, her long blond hair streaking behind her. Nancy was relieved that Claudia pulled up on her Vespa just then, too. She dropped it on the ground, not even pausing to put the kickstand down, and ran after Bess.

Paola's face twisted as she realized she was surrounded. Swiftly she ran past Nancy and into the arena.

Nancy took up the chase. "She's on her way in," she yelled into her walkie-talkie. "Someone call the police!" Paola was headed toward the walkway around the maze under the arena floor in the center of the amphitheater, her high heels clattering over the uneven ground. Even though Nancy was gaining on her, Paola was still several yards ahead as she reached the arena floor.

Glancing upward, Nancy could see Mick and Sandro bounding down from the sloping stands toward the maze. Paola saw them, too, and picked up her pace. But the wire fence that had blocked the teens' way the day before was looming in front of her.

Paola didn't even pause at the fence. Kicking off her shoes, she began climbing.

Nancy remembered Sandro's words about tourists getting hopelessly lost in the blocked-off area. Well, she wasn't going to let Paola lose her again, Nancy thought grimly.

With a burst of energy she launched herself at the fence and grabbed Paola's leg. Paola shook her leg violently, still trying to climb, but Nancy held on. Grabbing Paola's leg with both hands, Nancy let her feet drop away from the fence so that her entire body weight would pull Paola down.

It worked. Paola's hands slipped off the fence, and she began to fall, taking Nancy with her.

Then suddenly Paola jammed her foot into the fence, throwing both of them sideways over the safety railing. They were falling into the stone maze below!

Nancy hit the ground on her side, driving her elbow into her ribs. She rolled, trying to lessen the impact of her fall, and found herself facedown in the dirt. Gasping, she drew a ragged breath.

Nearby, Paola was lying where she had fallen, moving feebly. Her bag was on the ground beside her. Nancy forced herself to her knees and reached for Paola's bag, but Paola saw her and grabbed it away. She landed a bare foot in Nancy's chest that sent her sprawling. Then, struggling to her feet, Paola staggered down the passage. She rounded a corner and disappeared.

Nancy bounced back onto her feet with a groan. She looked up, trying to see over the high stone walls around her. The two guys were still making their way down the stands. Claudia and Bess were nowhere to be seen. Nancy hoped they were calling the police.

Hearing Paola's heavy breathing off to her right, Nancy headed toward the sound. They were playing cat and mouse, and the mouse had the advantage, Nancy realized as she leaned against a wall. Sandro had said there were tunnels for water around the side of the arena floor. If Paola knew that, too, she'd probably head for the edge of the maze. But where was she now?

"Go left and take your first right." Nancy jumped at the sound of Mick's voice coming from the walkie-talkie tucked in her waistband. She had forgotten that she had left it on. She looked up to see Mick standing in the stadium, waving and pointing.

He could see Paola, Nancy realized. Relief coursed through her body. All she had to do was follow his directions.

Paola must have heard Mick's voice, too, because Nancy heard her scramble through a nearby passage.

"She's running parallel to you, about twenty-five feet in front," Mick told Nancy. "Don't take your next right, it's a dead end. Take the one after that."

Sandro was racing down the stands, taking the stone steps two at a time. He was going to reach the fence any minute. Nancy almost grinned with relief as she saw her backup working.

"Double back!" Mick ordered. "Right and right again!" Nancy did as she was told and found herself in a small square area with an exit on her left. She took a wide turn and went through it.

Paola was ahead of her, headed for the edge of the arena floor, as Nancy had guessed. In a moment she would be inside the tunnels and out of Mick's view!

Then Nancy saw a figure hurtling over the fence and into the passage in front of Paola. It was Sandro! Giving a yell, he tackled Paola, and the two of them went down, rolling in the dust. A few more steps brought Nancy to them. She yanked Paola's bag away from her and sat down, still breathing hard.

Opening it, Nancy found a velvet bag. Inside it were Signor Andreotti's necklace, Signora De Luca's pin, and the Etruscan necklace that had started the whole adventure!

Mick's voice joined them in the maze. "Good work," he said cheerfully. "The police are entering the Colosseum now!"

"At least they let me out on bail," Sandro said. He skipped a few steps along the platform of Rome's central railroad station.

Claudia took his hand and squeezed it, smiling encouragingly at her boyfriend.

The two of them had accompanied Nancy, Bess, and Mick to the train that would take the three friends to Brindisi, a port city on the Adriatic Sea. From there they would catch a ferry to Athens. "Now at least I have a chance to redeem myself during the trial," Sandro continued. "If Nancy and Bess hadn't come along, I'd be sitting in jail for the rest of my life."

"We are still not sure what is going to happen," Claudia reminded him. "And your mother was not very happy."

Nancy could see the shame in Sandro's eyes. "At least she got her necklace back," he said softly. "I'm relieved that Paola kept it all this time. Apparently even *she* couldn't bring herself to sell the necklace of a good friend."

"But the two pieces Mr. Azar managed to smuggle out of the country still haven't been recovered," Nancy pointed out. "If they are, you'll get a much lighter sentence. Also, they should go easier on you because you helped capture Paola and Mr. Azar."

"I was wrong to do what I did," Sandro said. "I can't feel sorry for myself."

"Well, I for one feel sorry for Karine," Bess put in. "Her father's going to be in jail for a long time. Paola's confession clinched that for sure. I guess she couldn't bear to be the only one facing centuries in jail."

Nancy remembered Karine's reaction when she found out what happened and how her father had used her. Her anger and hurt had been so genuine that Nancy had no doubts that Karine had had no idea of what her father and Paola were doing.

"I feel sorry for Karine, too," Claudia added. "But she is a strong girl. And she has Massimo to help her through it."

"Massimo the charmer." Bess sighed. "If he hadn't had a crush on me and given me that necklace in the first place, none of this would have happened. No more romances for me, thank you! And no more Etruscan necklaces, fake or otherwise!"

Claudia laughed. "It was such a short time ago," she said. "And you are leaving already."

"We stayed an extra week," Nancy protested. "You've dragged us to every church and museum and restaurant in Rome."

"Well, you needed a vacation. You were all beat up from that chase in the Colosseum," Claudia insisted.

"You did a great job," Nancy assured her. "I'm

completely relaxed. But George will never forgive us if we leave her in Greece any longer."

"Where's Mick?" Bess asked as other passengers streamed past them. "If he doesn't hurry, we'll have to leave him behind."

"He just went to get us snacks for the trip. He'll be right back," Nancy told her.

"Probably running the whole way." Claudia's eyes gleamed. "After all, he begged to go to Greece with you every day, Nancy, until you finally gave in. You can bet he will not miss this train!"

Nancy hoped the others didn't notice the blush she felt rising to her cheeks. She waved as she caught sight of Mick down the platform. He waved back and broke into a jog.

"See?" Claudia asked. "Have fun in Greece and get some rest," she said, kissing Nancy, Mick, and Bess goodbye. "No more mysteries."

"No way," Bess agreed. "No romances and no Greek jewelry," she said firmly. "In fact, if it keeps us out of trouble, I won't even shop!"

After Sandro and Claudia had left Nancy felt Mick's arms creep around her waist. He turned her to face him.

"Should we play by Bess's rules?" he asked with a lazy grin. "No romances?"

A warm feeling spread through Nancy as she gazed into his green eyes. "Maybe one romance," she murmured, raising her lips to meet his.

Concluding the Passport to Romance Trilogy:

Nancy, Bess, and George have found heaven on earth: the soft breezes, clear waters, and warm sun of the Greek isles. But beneath the gentle surface of the storied wine-dark sea lurks a violent undertow. Nancy discovers that the mythic playground of Apollo, Aphrodite, and Athena has turned into a testing ground for terrorists!

Three passports, including Bess's, have been stolen from their hotel, and Nancy suspects they have fallen into the hands of international fugitives. Determined to identify their island accomplice, she learns just how desperate and deadly the terrorists are. For *they* are determined to bring Nancy's summer in Europe to a sudden—and tragic—end . . . in *GREEK ODYSSEY*, Case #74 in the Nancy Drew Files™.